SECOND CHANCE CHRISTMAS

A PINE HILLS NOVELLA

PINE HILLS SERIES
BOOK ONE

LARAMIE CUMMINGS

ISBN: 979-8-218-61684-7

ISBN: 978-1-967594-00-9

First Publication: 2024

Cover design by: Get Covers, getcovers.com

Publisher: WYde Open Pages, WY, USA, owner@wydeopenpages.com

Printed in the United States of America

www.llcummingsbooks.com

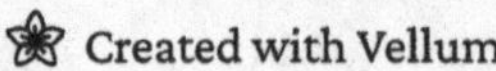 Created with Vellum

To everyone who believes in second and third chances.

A NOTE TO MY READERS

Your well-being and mental health are important to me. This story touches on some themes that may be difficult for some readers. If the topics below are something you feel challenging, please take care of yourself as you decide whether to continue. It's okay to step away or skip parts of the story if you need to. Your comfort and peace come first.

Trigger Warnings:

- Death of a parent - Cancer diagnosis of a parent - Depictions of grief and loss - Alcohol consumption - Heart Attack - Use of profanity

PROLOGUE

My senior year of high school was supposed to be perfect. This was the year to achieve my dreams by having fun, getting accepted to my top choice for college, and hopefully being in a relationship with Lane. Instead, Lane decimated me that year.

I believed we were on the cusp of something incredible. A lifetime of friendship had grown into something electric, and I thought we were finally ready to embrace it. Lane was my person. I knew all his quirks, his habits, the little things that made him *him*. As our friendship blurred into flirting, I couldn't stop myself from dreaming about what came next.

We were both heading to New York for college—me to Columbia, him to NYU. Sure, the schools were different, but they were close enough that I thought we'd still be us. Everything felt perfect. It was all clicking into place. Until it all fell apart.

Lane disappeared for a week without explanation, avoiding me like I was a problem he didn't want to solve. At first, I tried to convince myself he was just busy, that there had to be a reason for the sudden silence. But when Sheera cornered me in the hallway, her voice dripping with smug satisfaction, I learned the truth: Lane had been badmouthing me behind my back, laughing about how I was pining over him while he hung out with his track buddies and "kept his options open."

When Lane finally showed up to talk, my anger was volcanic. I was pacing, rehearsing every cutting thing I wanted to say, and then there he was, acting like nothing had happened. "What's the matter, Pipes?" he asked, feigning concern.

That question snapped the last thread holding me together.

"You know, Lane, I always thought you were the nicest person in my life," I began, my voice shaking. "You were my best friend. And when I fell for you, I thought you were falling for me, too. But I guess I was just a fool."

"What are you talking about? What's going on?" His confusion only stoked my rage.

"Avoiding me for a week is bad enough, but you didn't even have the decency to tell me why. Instead, I had to hear from Sheera that you've been laughing at me. Laughing at me, Lane! Did you think I wouldn't find out? Did you think I wouldn't realize you're just another asshole who uses people and throws them away when it's inconvenient?"

"Piper, I—"

"No." I cut him off, shaking my head as tears blurred my vision. "Don't. Just don't. Go fuck yourself, Lane. I never want to see or hear from you again."

I didn't wait for a response. I turned and ran as fast as my legs would carry me, my chest burning with betrayal and heartbreak.

The summer that followed was a blur of heat, tears, and long afternoons where I couldn't figure out if I was angry, devastated, or just plain numb. My best friends, Bri, and Samuel, became my lifeline. They showed up at my house the day after the fight, armed with snacks, trashy movies, and all the righteous fury I couldn't summon myself.

"Alright, Pipes," Bri announced, tossing her overnight bag onto my bed with dramatic flair. "You're allowed to wallow for three days, max. After that, we're doing face masks, and you're getting back out there. Agreed?"

I didn't have the energy to argue. Sam followed her lead, holding up a bag of my favorite pastries like a peace offering. "She's serious, you know. You can wallow, but we're not letting you sink."

True to their word, they didn't. For the rest of senior year and the summer, Bri, and Sam dragged me out of my funk every time it threatened to pull me under. Some days, that meant sprawling on Bri's couch, binge-watching *Buffy the Vampire Slayer* while she narrated every scene like a sports commentator. Other days, it meant Sam hauling me out of bed for early morning hikes, claiming fresh air would "reset my chakras," even though neither of us believed in chakras.

We spent entire afternoons at the bookstore, sipping iced lattes and coming up with ridiculous challenges—like how many romance novels we could stack before the tower fell or who could find the weirdest book title in the store. Bri orchestrated "Piper Nights," evenings dedicated to distracting me from my heartbreak. One night, we went roller skating under glittering disco lights, Sam attempting—and failing—an impressive spin move. Another night, we stayed up until 3 a.m., crafting a playlist of songs for crying sessions and dance parties in the kitchen.

But for all their efforts, the quiet moments still hit the hardest. Late at night, I'd lie in bed replaying that awful fight with Lane in my head, wondering how years of friendship had unraveled in minutes.

By August, though, the knots in my chest loosened just enough for me to breathe without shattering. Bri and Sam were relentless in reminding me of the future waiting for me at Columbia.

"New York City, Pipes," Sam said one night as we sat on my porch, eating ice cream straight out of the cartons. "You're about to be living the dream—skyscrapers, magical pizza, and, let's not forget, cute college guys who aren't assholes named Lane."

Bri grinned, holding up her spoon in a toast. "To new beginnings!"

I smiled, clinking my spoon against hers. "To new beginnings."

I hadn't fully healed when I packed my bags for Columbia. Heartbreak doesn't work that way. But thanks to Bri, Sam, and a summer filled with love and laughter, I was ready to take that first step forward.

CHAPTER ONE
PIPER

Fifteen years later...

The Christmas season had turned out to be a cataclysmic fuck storm—one catastrophe after another—and I was barely keeping afloat. A mountainous stack of holiday orders loomed over me. Great for business, sure, but suffocating all the same. November used to be my prep month for December; now it was as chaotic as the holidays themselves. October? Forget about enjoying crisp air and pumpkins. That was my new prep month, eaten alive by spreadsheets and stocking lists. This year, my bookstore, Bennett's Books, was busier than ever. Online orders poured in by the minute, and the shop itself saw a steady flow of customers.

I'd even managed to rent out all five studio apartments above the store on HomeBnB for the entire New Year—a first. I should've been thrilled. After all, things were going well, and everyone expected me to be jumping for joy. Business was booming and I was raking in more money than ever before. Christmas cheer surrounded me at every turn.

But I couldn't feel any of it.

Not this year. This year was a freight train of misery that had smashed into my life and dragged me, screaming, through hell.

Bennett's Books had always been my heart and soul, my haven. My grandpa built it for my grandma—a gift for her insatiable love of books and the adventures they brought her. A romantic at heart, he created a bookstore where she could live in the stories she adored. It was their shared dream, later passed down to my dad.

For him, Bennett's Books was more than a livelihood; it was his passion, his third love. First came my mom. Then me. My dad and I spent countless hours wandering its shelves, reading aloud from our favorite novels, sipping hot cocoa from my mom's coffee shop two doors down. Our lives—our memories—were woven into the walls of that store.

I had it all back then. A loving family. My goofy Newfie, Sasha. And Greg, my boyfriend of eight years. We'd met in grad school—me pursuing an MFA, him chasing a law degree. We returned to Pine Hills to build a life together. I'd been ready for the next steps: a home, maybe even kids. Life was perfect.

Until it wasn't.

In January, my mom was diagnosed with breast cancer. It was a gut punch to our family, but we rallied around her, fighting for her health. Trips to New York City for treatments became routine. In July, my parents made one such trip a mini-vacation—a Broadway show, dinner out, an attempt to lift her spirits.

But it didn't go as planned.

That night, after the show, my dad started feeling unwell. My mother acted fast and decided they needed to go to urgent care. Once they stepped into the elevator, he collapsed while clutching his chest. A heart attack. By the time the doors opened, he was gone.

Just like that, my dad was dead, leaving a gaping black hole where he should've been. Losing him shattered me, my mom, my grandparents—our entire world. Grief swallowed my mom whole. She lost her will to fight the cancer, retreating into herself while I scrambled to hold everything together: her care, the family businesses, the endless logistics that follow a death. The summer blurred into exhaustion and despair.

By October, I clawed my way out of the fog and threw myself into preparing for the holidays. The bookstore demanded my attention, and my grandpa—grieving in his own suppressed way—leaned on me more than ever. Together, we propped each other up as best we could.

Then Greg dealt me another blow by deciding that he couldn't handle it anymore.

According to him, I'd "changed too much" after my dad's death. He didn't "blame me" but said he couldn't live in my grief bubble. A breakup was devastating enough. But then I discovered the real reason behind it: Greg had been cheating on me since February with another lawyer he'd met at a Vegas conference. I found out through a sext that popped up on my iPad—still synced to his account. Katrina. That was her name. Their text history told me everything I needed to know.

That betrayal broke me.

I spiraled. I hated myself for being blind, for letting my life unravel in every way. The year had chewed me up and spit me out, leaving me a hollow shell of who I once was.

But I wasn't completely lost.

The bookstore, my family, and my friends kept me grounded. My grandparents, my best friends Bri and Samuel, and my dog Sasha were my lifelines. Once a week, we gathered at Bennett's Books for wine and venting. Surrounded by love and laughter, I felt a flicker of normalcy. They reminded me why I kept fighting, why I got out of bed each morning. They, and the hope that someday my mom would come back to me, made me ready to live again.

Snapping out of my reverie, I stared at the endless list of online, pick-up, and restocking orders waiting for me. Maybe next year would be better. Maybe happiness would return.

But for now? This year could fucking suck it.

CHAPTER TWO
PIPER

Even though I was battling depression, I found some comfort in the chaos of my work. Running the bookstore, managing my HomeBnB rentals, and learning the ropes to eventually inherit my grandparents' company kept me busy. Bennett's Corporation oversaw a variety of businesses, and while I wasn't particularly enthusiastic about all of them, my grandpa had set up a structure that relied on incredible managers to keep things running. That left him, my grandma, aunt and I be able to pay attention to the best parts: the bookstore, the coffee shop, and the flower shop.

I was trying to stay focused, resisting the urge to open a bottle of wine while deciphering the next online order on my screen, when the shop bell chimed. Someone had walked in, and I heard a faint "hello" from the front.

Lola, my one staff member, was on a short break, so I called out, "Hello! I'm coming. Just give me two seconds!"

I hurried through the curtain that separated the back from the front desk and immediately froze.

A tall, broad-chested man stood before me. His presence

seemed to fill the entire room, and when I looked up, my heart lodged itself firmly in my throat.

Could my life get any worse?

He stared at me with an intensity that made my skin prickle. His deep brown eyes locked onto mine, and his dark chestnut hair looked annoyingly perfect. Then, he spoke.

"Hey there, Piper. I don't know if you remember me, but we went to high school together. It's me, Lane. I-uh—"

"I remember." My voice came out rough, sharp—like a blade I couldn't control. "It's been a long time. How can I help you, Lane?"

My words were clipped, my tone bordering on rude. Because, of course, it was Lane Schiller—the boy who'd shattered my heart in high school. Lane, with his easy smile and effortless charm, the one every girl (and guy) had a crush on. He was the kindest person I'd ever known—or so I thought until he became the first person to truly break me.

"Well, uh, yeah. I remember you too," he said awkwardly, shoving his hands into his jacket pockets.He seemed to not know what to say next.

The silence that followed was starting to border along excruciating. I glared at him, waiting to see if he had anything meaningful to say. Seconds dragged into what felt like an eternity of awkwardness.

Thankfully, Sasha came barreling out of the back to save us both. My massive, goofy Newfoundland ran straight up to Lane—and shoved her nose directly into his butt.

"Oh my god, Sasha!" I cried, mortified. "Stop!"

Lane laughed, startled but not upset, as I tried to pull her away. "I am *so* sorry," I stammered. "She only sniffs the butts of people she likes."

"Well, Sasha," Lane said with a grin, crouching down to pet her, "you must like me, huh? You're a pretty girl, aren't you?"

Sasha responded by licking his face, and I couldn't help but stare. Damn it. He was still gorgeous, and my stupid brain betrayed me for half a second, wishing I could lick his face, too.

"Um, yeah. Sorry about her," I managed. "As you can see, Sasha's the best girl—but maybe a little too friendly sometimes."

"It's fine. I love dogs. And she *is* a beaut," he said, still scratching her ears as she wagged her massive tail.

He stood, his hands brushing his jeans, and cleared his throat. "Anyway, I'm here for my room. The note said to check in at the bookstore's front desk. Can you point me to whoever handles that?"

"Oh!" I blinked, startled. "That'd be me. I'm the owner." My voice had gone rigid again, clipped and professional. "But I don't recall seeing your name on my HomeBnB list. Let me double-check."

I grabbed my laptop, frowning as I opened the booking page. There was only one guest checking into my luxury suite, and they'd reserved it for a long stay to work on their next novel.

"Uh, Piper—wait," Lane interjected. "You might have me down as Lance Sterling. Or, um, L. Sterling. My assistant made the reservation and probably used my pen name."

I turned to stare at him, utterly dumbfounded.

"Wait. *You're* L. Sterling?" My voice came out louder than I intended, laced with disbelief.

He rubbed the back of his neck, looking sheepish. "Yeah. That'd be me."

"You're *the* L. Sterling? The author of *Catch Me Now* and *Rural Love*? The guy who's written dozens of books and articles?"

"Uh... yes?" His answer was hesitant, his eyes darting to mine like he wasn't sure what reaction to expect.

"Holy *shit*, Lane." I let out a disbelieving laugh, one hand gripping the counter for support. "I thought you were a *woman*! You write *romance*, for crying out loud!"

He smirked, clearly amused. "I take it you've read my work?"

"Read your work? Are you kidding me? I *love* your books! *Catch Me Now* and *Rural Love* are two of my all-time favorites. But now..." My voice faltered as my brain caught up with my words.

"Now what?" he asked, raising an eyebrow.

"Now I'm rethinking everything, because *Lane Schiller*—the guy who broke my heart—is my favorite author? That's just..." I trailed off, staring at him. "I can't believe this. I hate you, Lane. I can't like your work anymore. I *detest* you."

He blinked, stunned, as I rambled on.

"This is some sick cosmic joke. My favorite author is *you*. And now you're staying here? In my HomeBnB? This year just keeps getting worse."

I grabbed my water bottle from under the counter and took a long drink—except it wasn't water. It was wine. Did I care? Nope. I chugged it anyway.

"Is that wine?" Lane asked, his voice calm, almost amused.

"Mmm hmm," I mumbled around the bottle, still drinking. I knew some wine had dribbled out of my mouth as I chugged.

"You okay?"

"Uh, uh," I muttered, shaking my head as I drained the last of the bottle.

Setting it down with a thud, I wiped my mouth and glared at him. "You're L. Sterling, and you're staying in my HomeBnB. Fine. Let's go upstairs."

I motioned for him to follow me to the back staircase. If he could pretend we didn't have a messy history, then damn it, so could I.

CHAPTER THREE
LANE

I didn't follow Piper right away. Watching her chug a Hydro Flask of wine after her little freakout, then spin on her heel like nothing happened, left me stunned. And, honestly, a little amused. She was still the same Piper Bennett—chaotic, funny, and completely unpredictable.

I couldn't help but remember how much I'd missed her sharp wit and wild energy. High school memories flickered in my mind like an old film reel, interspersed with glimpses of her from over the years. I tried to shake them off.

What I couldn't shake was how stunning she still was. Time had only made her more beautiful. Her brown hair framed her face in soft waves, her eyes—still that warm, earthy brown—were full of fire. She had the same flushed cheeks I remembered, though now framed by reading glasses. She wore an oversized green sweater and black leggings, an effortless combination that somehow made her look... perfect.

It took me a moment to snap out of it and realize she was already halfway up the stairs. I hurried after her, lugging my duffle and laptop bag, following her through the shop's charming, old wooden staircase.

The stairs had always been a favorite feature of mine growing up. Now, decorated for Christmas with garland, red bows, and soft white lights, they were even more magical. The building was from the late 1800s, and Piper's family had owned it for generations. Her dad had renovated it a few years back, modernizing it without losing its charm. I remembered stopping in then to pick up a book for my niece. Piper's dad had given me a proud tour of the space.

Now I was climbing those stairs with Piper, heading to my new temporary home. I'd learned about her HomeBnB while searching for a quiet place to finish my novel. Pine Hills seemed like the perfect escape after years of burnout in New York City. The city had taken its toll on me, draining my creativity and leaving me yearning for something... calmer.

This wasn't just about writing. My sister and her family lived nearby, and I aspired to be more present for them, especially my niece and nephew. Being the "cool uncle" sounded a hell of a lot better than endless nights in a Manhattan apartment that felt more like a box than a home.

Maureen, the woman I'd been seeing before I left, had only added to my restlessness. She was a brilliant, powerhouse lawyer who thrived in the relentless energy of New York. And while I cared for her, staying with her—or in the city—felt stagnant. She fit perfectly into the fast-paced chaos. I didn't anymore.

Piper led me down a cozy hallway with oak paneling and green, patterned wallpaper that made the space feel warm and inviting. It didn't feel like a guest accommodation; it felt like home.

When we reached the end of the hall, she stopped in front of a door.

"This is you," she said, handing me a key. "The binder inside has everything you need—Wi-Fi info, house rules, local recommendations. There's a QR code for your phone if you prefer digital. I live across the hall, so if you have an emergency, you can knock or find me downstairs. My cell's on the website and in the binder too."

"Um…" I hesitated, not wanting her to leave just yet. "Do you want to come in and show me around?"

She raised an eyebrow, clearly weighing her options.

"Do you *need* me to show you around?"

"Yes. I do."

She sighed, unlocking the door and pushing it open. I followed her inside, taking in the space.

It was more than a room—it was an incredible studio loft. The exposed brick and oak details gave it a rustic charm, while large windows let in soft natural light. The kitchen was fully equipped, the living area was cozy, and the king-sized bed looked ridiculously comfortable.

What caught my attention most was the writing desk by the largest window. It overlooked a courtyard—an old alleyway repurposed into a charming garden and patio space.

"This is amazing," I said, running my hand over the smooth wood of the desk and gazing out the window. "Your dad did an incredible job with this place."

I glanced back at Piper, and my heart sank at the sadness in her expression.

"Yeah," she said softly. "He did."

Her voice was strained, and I immediately regretted bringing him up. Did her and her dad have a strained relationship? Before I could say anything, she cleared her throat. "So, do you need anything else? Or can I go?"

Her words were rushed, but I could see she was holding something back.

"Uh, I just have a few questions," I said, not wanting her to leave yet.

She closed her eyes and took a deep breath, visibly steadying herself. "Fine."

"Is there anything I should know about the place? Like quirks or things that don't work?"

"No. It's all good. My handyman checked everything, and the room was deep cleaned before you arrived." She hesitated before adding, "I even got a special writing desk for you. I didn't know it was *you* when I bought it, but I knew L. Sterling was coming and figured you'd need a pleasant space to write."

"You didn't have to do that," I said, touched. "Thanks, Pipes."

Her eyes flashed with annoyance. "It's Piper," she said firmly.

"Sorry."

The air between us shifted, the tension palpable. Her gaze was a mix of anger and sadness, and it hit me like a punch to the gut. Memories of high school—of how I'd hurt her—came rushing back.

"Well," I said awkwardly, "if I need anything, I know where to find you. Thanks, Piper."

She said nothing, just turned and walked out, slamming the door behind her.

I stood there, stunned. What the hell had I done? It felt like my very presence had ruined her day, but I couldn't understand why.

Surely she wasn't still upset about high school. Was she?

Acting on impulse, I ran to the door and flung it open. "Piper!" I called down the hall. She was nearly at the stairs when she stopped and turned.

"What?"

"Maybe *Rural Love* and *Catch Me Now* were written for you." I gave her a wink and shut the door before she could respond, my heart pounding.

Why did I feel the need to say that?

CHAPTER FOUR
PIPER

I bolted down to my office, heart pounding. What the hell just happened? Was Lane messing with me? I pressed my forehead against the door and gave it a few gentle thuds. *Why? Why? Why?*

Within ten minutes, I'd experienced an overwhelming cocktail of emotions: shock, rage, nostalgia—and, annoyingly, lust. Lane Schiller was always hot, so that part wasn't surprising. But finding out he was L. Sterling? That had sent me reeling.

For weeks, I'd assumed L. Sterling was a woman. The mental whiplash of discovering it was Lane—my high school obsession, first love, and first heartbreak—had left me raw. And now he was here, staying in my HomeBnB for months. Not just here, but right across the hall. Unavoidable.

Before everything fell apart, Lane had been a constant in my life. Our families were close, so we grew up together. I'd been hopelessly, stupidly in love with him for years. But after he shattered my heart, I'd cut him out completely. I avoided him so thoroughly that every time I heard he was visiting Pine Hills, I'd make myself scarce—fleeing the town like I was being hunted.

Looking back, I probably should have just faced him sooner. It would have saved me a small fortune in travel expenses and a lot of sleepless nights wondering what I'd say if I ever ran into him.

And now, after all this time, here he was.

Seeing him again hadn't been as catastrophic as I'd feared. Honestly, it had gone better than expected—if you ignored the part where I told him I hated him. Still, I needed a plan. I couldn't let him distract me. The best strategy was to avoid him entirely for the next few weeks. But how was I supposed to manage that when we were sharing the same building?

As I leaned against the door, lost in thought, a knock startled me so badly I let out a shriek. My heart plummeted. I *knew* it was Lane before I even opened the door.

I took a deep breath, steeling myself, and turned the knob.

And there he was. All six-foot-something of him, with his ruffled brown hair, warm brown eyes, and that damn perfectly trimmed beard. His long-sleeved navy blue shirt clung to his muscular frame, and I cursed the flutter in my stomach. He looked good. Too good.

I realized I was staring and quickly closed my gaping mouth.

"Uh, hi," I said, trying to keep my tone neutral. "Can I help you with something?"

"Yes," he said, running a hand through his hair. He looked... nervous. "I was wondering if we could talk."

"About what?" I crossed my arms, trying to ignore the heat building inside me.

"Well—uh—can I come in?"

I hesitated but nodded. "Sure. Come in."

I led him into my small, cozy office, motioning for him to sit at the chair in front of my desk. He did, fidgeting slightly.

"So, Lane," I said, trying to sound casual but knowing I came off cold. "What's on your mind? It's been years since we last talked."

"Yeah," he said with a sheepish smile. "It's been a while."

An awkward silence followed. He stared at me, and I stared right back, trying not to let the tension get to me. My cheeks felt warm, and I hated that my body betrayed me like this. Finally, he broke eye contact, looking out the window as if searching for the right words.

"Look," he began, "I know things ended... badly between us. But I'm here to work on my book and get some clarity. I'm also thinking about moving back. This isn't an ideal situation, I get that. But I need this. I need a break from the city, and this seemed like the perfect place to figure things out. So I was wondering..." He trailed off, meeting my eyes again. "Could we start fresh? Let bygones be bygones and maybe try to be friends?"

I stared at him, processing his words. And then I exploded.

"*Let bygones be bygones?*" I repeated, throwing my hands up. "Sure. Why not? Breaking my heart is no big deal. Ancient history, right?" I laughed bitterly. "Fine. Let's start over."

I walked around the desk, stopping right in front of him. With one hand on my hip and the other pointing accusingly at him, I glared. "But let me make this *very* clear, Lane. I don't want to 'start fresh' as friends. What I want is for us to be cordial. We'll live in proximity, and I'll do all the neighborly bullshit. But we will *never* be friends again."

I took a step back, folding my arms across my chest. "Now, if you don't mind, I have a shop to run. So, if we're done here, I'd appreciate it if you left."

Lane didn't move at first. He just looked at me with those infuriatingly beautiful brown eyes, like he was trying to see straight through me.

"Neighbors it is, then," he finally said, his voice quiet.

He stood and walked out without another word.

I let out a frustrated sigh, immediately regretting how I'd handled that. I hadn't even let him finish before blurting out my rage. Now I was irritated at myself for letting Lane Schiller crawl under my skin.

Why was I still letting him affect me after all these years? I should have been over this by now. But as I stood there, the old sadness crept in, mingling with anger and regret. My heart ached, and memories of my first love—and my first heartbreak—rushed back like a tidal wave.

CHAPTER FIVE
LANE

I'd been back in Pine Hills for two weeks, and I was already struggling. Two weeks, and all I had to show for it was a single chapter of complete and utter garbage. Inspiration had evaded me, and without it, I couldn't write.

I'd mostly confined myself to my room during this time, venturing out only to meet my sister's family, grab food, or stock up on booze. The rest of the time? I was a couch potato.

I binged trash TV and Netflix—something I never used to do. I didn't exercise, breaking a streak I'd kept since my senior year of high school. I ate an embarrassing amount of junk food. I spent time playing mindless games on my phone.

And I avoided Piper like the plague.

She had made it clear that she'd be "neighborly" and nothing more. True to her word, whenever we crossed paths, she was polite but distant. One time, we both stepped out of our places at the same time, and I gestured for her to walk ahead of me to the downstairs. She gave me a quick smile, a "Thanks," and continued on her way with Sasha.

Her words still stung. They had dredged up the past, and I

couldn't shake the thought of how I'd imagined our lives might turn out. For years, I'd believed Piper, and I had an undeniable connection, like some invisible thread tethered us together. She had always been on my mind, no matter where life took me.

But her sharp words in her office had hit harder than I expected.

To my surprise, though, Sasha, Piper's dog, had become an unexpected source of comfort.

It started with faint scratching at my door in the first week. I ignored it at first, but it kept happening. When I finally checked, I found Sasha sitting patiently outside.

From then on, it became a routine. Every day around 2 p.m., Sasha would scratch at my door. I'd let her in, give her a treat, and we'd cuddle on the couch while I half-watched whatever nonsense was on TV. By 3:30, like clockwork, she'd head back out. None the wiser that she'd brightened my day.

It was like our little secret. Piper couldn't know her dog was sneaking in daily cuddles with me.

By the end of two weeks, I knew I couldn't keep Netflix and chilling. The last two weeks had been the break I didn't know I needed—my first real downtime in over a decade. But I was feeling the itch to be a storyteller again.

Determined to turn things around, I showered, got dressed, and headed downstairs to the bookstore. I hoped that Piper and I might exchange more than a passing "hello" this time. For some reason, today felt different.

When I reached the bottom of the stairs, Sasha was the first to greet me. I crouched down, giving her an enthusiastic belly rub.

As I finished, I caught Piper watching us from behind the counter.

"Sasha and you seem close," she said, her tone tinged with curiosity—and maybe a hint of jealousy. Did she suspect our daily cuddle sessions?

"What can I say? We're best friends now," I replied with a grin.

"I can see that." Her brows furrowed slightly. "So, what are your plans today, Lane?"

Her question caught me off guard. I'd expected to be the one making the first move, but here she was, starting a conversation. I had to tread lightly, not wanting to scare her off. It was like she was a wild animal and I had to approach lightly.

"I'm planning to write," I said, leaning casually against the counter. "We'll see how it goes. Haven't had much inspiration lately. What about you?"

"I've got work. Maybe some stuff for my grandpa regarding the other businesses. Nothing glamorous. Wait—" She tilted her head. "You *haven't* been writing this whole time?"

Her surprise made me falter.

"Well, no. I've been doing... nothing, really. Watching trash TV and eating trash food. Today's my first day trying to get back into it."

"I assumed you were in some kind of writing bubble," she said, her expression softening.

"More like a writing jail cell," I joked.

That earned a small smile. "Interesting term," she said. "Why a jail cell?"

"I came here for inspiration. I was drained—completely burned out—and I needed a break from the city. These past two weeks have been the first actual break I've had in years. No stories, no editing, no marketing. Just... quiet."

"Interesting," she said again.

"You must think I'm the most fascinating man alive," I teased. "You keep saying that."

She snorted. "You've never not been interesting, Lane."

The words hung in the air between us, and I wanted to press

further, to peel back the layers of what she meant. But before I could, she broke the silence.

"Anyway, I'm heading to Crestview for lunch. I do this every Wednesday—take Sasha, eat, hike, maybe read at a coffee shop. Want to join me?"

She looked as surprised by her own invitation as I felt. I couldn't help but say yes.

"I'd like that. What time?"

"10:30. Meet me here?"

"Perfect. See you then."

As I walked to the coffee shop, nerves prickled at me. This wasn't just a casual outing—it felt like a step forward.

At the shop, Piper's grandmother, Mrs. Bennett, greeted me warmly.

"Oh, Lane dear! Sit down, and I'll bring you a sausage biscuit. Would you like a blueberry muffin, too? Piper loves them with butter!"

Her warmth was infectious, and as I ate, we caught up.

"Lane, spend time with Piper," she said after hearing about my plans. "She needs it. Since her mom's cancer and losing her dad, she hasn't been the same. She's a shell of herself."

My heart sank. Piper's mom had cancer? Her dad had passed away? How hadn't I known?

I sat in stunned silence, grief washing over me. I should have noticed. The signs had been there—her bluntness, her wine-chugging, the cloud of sadness that seemed to follow her.

But now wasn't the time to dwell. I needed to be present for her, to make this day in Crestview a bright spot for both of us.

At 10:30 sharp, I closed my laptop and headed back to the bookstore. Piper deserved this break—and maybe I did, too.

CHAPTER SIX
PIPER

All morning, I've been like that Eminem song—knees weak, palms sweaty, arms heavy. I almost vomited, but not because of Mom's spaghetti. It was thanks to a weird bout of insanity where I invited Lane to join me on a trip to Crestview.

I groaned, replaying it in my head. The moment to leave was approaching fast, and Lane would be coming along with Sasha and me. Sasha's presence would help ease the awkwardness, but I still felt like an idiot. I'd blurted out the invitation, and now I was annoyed with myself. Well, no—if I was being honest, I was nervous.

The last two weeks of Lane living across from me hadn't been terrible. He'd said little to me, and I to him, but I'd had plenty of chances to *look*. My loathing for him had dulled into something more tolerable. Was that progress?

As if on cue, Lane strolled in, and my stomach flipped. Or maybe it dropped. I wasn't sure which.

"It's about damn time," I blurted out. "Let's hit the road, Joe! This is Sasha's favorite day of the week."

Grabbing my purse and keys off the counter, I strode toward the backroom door and out to my car. Lane followed close behind, murmuring just loud enough for me to hear, "I'd never make you wait, pretty girl."

The words were meant for Sasha, I told myself, but a traitorous part of me wished they were for me.

We climbed into the car. I glanced at him, and he looked right back at me, his steady gaze making my stomach do weird flips. Again.

"You don't have to come if you're busy," I said, fumbling nervously. "I mean, I'm sure you have better things to do—like being L. Sterling or whatever. Your life's probably way busier than mine. Are you sure you want to come? I mean, with come with us —me and Sasha?"

His brown eyes sparkled with amusement before softening into something warmer.

"Piper, I've been wanting to spend time with you since I got here."

The butterflies in my stomach morphed into something more like pterodactyls. My cheeks burned.

"Alright," I managed. "Let's go, then."

I started the car and pulled out of the driveway, Noah Kahan's voice filling the silence.

The drive began quietly, the music providing a comfortable background. Lane broke the silence first.

"So," he asked, clearing his throat, "what've you been up to since high school?"

I hesitated, unsure where to begin.

"Um, I went to college and got my degree in English," I said finally. "Then I got a master's. I even have an MFA I'm not using because I'm running the family business now. One day I'll take over everything, though I always wanted to write romance novels or children's books. Maybe someday. But you—you're the one living my dream as a bestselling romance author. I'm jealous."

I smirked at him before continuing, "I've had Sasha for three years, and she's the best friend I could ask for. I'm still close with Sam and Bri. That's my life in a nutshell. What about you?"

"I love Sam and Bri," he said with a grin. "Isn't Bri married now? And Sam was dating that guy in New York for a while. I met them a few times for drinks. Are they still together?"

I stared at him, startled. How did he know so much about my best friends? Had they really been in contact with Lane all this time?

Covering my shock, I nodded. "Yeah, I'm lucky to have them. Especially after this past year."

I cursed inwardly as the words left my mouth. I hadn't meant to let that slip. To cover my blunder, I teased in a low, god-like voice, "What about you, *Almighty New York Times Bestselling Author*?"

Lane chuckled. "Still as silly as ever, I see. Let's see... I also got an MFA. I wrote my first novel during undergrad and self-published it. A professor connected me with an agent, and before I knew it, I was publishing traditionally. I live in a little apartment on the Upper East Side now. Nothing too exciting."

"Nothing too exciting?!" I exclaimed. "You're living my dream! I've read all your books, including *Quiet Dawn*. That book blew me away. The spies, the banter, the twists—I couldn't believe a 20-year-old wrote something so complex."

Realizing I was rambling, I clamped my mouth shut.

Lane smirked. "You've read *all* my books? What about my short stories or articles?"

"Maybe," I muttered, cheeks burning.

His teasing grin widened. "Interesting, Piper Bennett. I thought you *hated* me?"

"Shut up, you ass. I don't think I said that," I huffed, swatting his arm.

Big mistake. His arm was solid muscle, and my hand betrayed me, giving it a squeeze.

Oh no. Did I just *squeeze* his arm? Why wouldn't my hand let go?

Lane laughed, a deep, warm sound. "I've worked hard for these guns."

I burst out laughing too, finally wrenching my hand away. "Your arms... they're so firm... and *big*," I gasped between giggles.

"You can feel them anytime," he said, grinning.

"Oh, I will. Maybe at the next book club meeting—with all the old ladies there."

Lane laughed, his gaze full of warmth and something else.

The rest of the ride flew by, filled with easy banter and talk of books and music. It felt strangely normal.

At the café, Lane listened intently as I recommended my favorite dishes. When the waitress flirted shamelessly with him, a flicker of jealousy bubbled in my chest.

"So, do girls drop their panties for you everywhere you go?" I blurted.

Lane looked surprised, but quickly recovered. "I've had my fair share of offers, but I'm not a player, Piper. I'm looking for something real."

His confession caught me off guard, stirring something I wasn't ready to examine.

Over beers and conversation, my walls crumbled. Lane listened, really listened, as I shared the challenges of the past year. He asked thoughtful questions, his sincerity disarming me.

By the time our food arrived, I realized he was holding my hand across the table.

And for the first time in a long time, I felt... lighter.

CHAPTER SEVEN

LANE

As our meal came to a close, I fell back into old habits with Piper. She opened up about her rough year, and I shared how I was looking to settle down and slow things down for once. We talked about the places we'd traveled to, the random things we'd done in our twenties, and the mundane stuff that only felt right when shared with someone you've known for years—world news, dumb jokes, little life updates.

When the check arrived, I didn't hesitate. I reached for it, ready to pay.

"Lane! I invited you. Let me pay," she protested, her voice sincere but firm.

"Nope. My treat. This has been a fun experience, Pipes." I said, forgetting for a second that I couldn't call her that anymore.

She shot me a look. "Fine, but I'm getting our after-hiking beer." She huffed, her eyes narrowing in playful defiance and not correcting me on her name.

"Fine," I smirked back.

After we left the café, we headed to the car to grab Sasha. There was a small trail off the main street that led to a peaceful walk, not really a hike, more like a long stroll through open fields and some quiet wooded areas. The air was crisp, and the ground had a light dusting of snow, though the cement path itself was mostly clear.

Walking beside Piper, bundled up with Sasha at our side, I felt something stir inside me—an idea, a story. I wasn't sure if it was the calm atmosphere, the quiet of the moment, or just being here with Piper, but I felt inspiration creeping in.

Piper broke the silence, her voice soft but filled with contentment. "I love this time of year. It's so peaceful right now. Sasha gets to run free and be off-leash. It's nice to escape life, even if just for an afternoon."

I smiled down at her, nudging my body gently against hers. "I agree. Today's been awesome. Thank you for inviting me. It might be exactly what I needed."

She stopped walking and turned to face me, her eyes wide as if something was warring inside her, some hesitation that she wasn't ready to let out. Then, after a beat, she spoke.

"It might have been what I needed too," she said quietly, her gaze locking with mine.

I felt the weight of her words, her muddy brown eyes drawing me in as they always had. It was like she was searching for something, but I couldn't tell what. Without thinking, my hand reached up to stroke her cheek. The touch was soft, almost instinctive, and I couldn't help myself.

"Piper," I murmured, my voice low, "I've always been so entranced by you. But right now, you look especially beautiful."

I don't know what came over me, but before I could second-guess it, I leaned down and kissed her lips gently.

Time seemed to stand still. Her lips were soft, warm, and a rush of calm washed over me as I felt her hands rest against my biceps. Then, as I deepened the kiss slightly, I felt her tense, and she pulled away.

Her cheeks were flushed, but this time, they were a deeper shade of red. "Lane. I—uh, wow."

She was speechless, and so was I. For a moment, the world felt like it had shifted, and neither of us knew what to say next. But I grabbed her hand, squeezing it gently, and we continued our walk. Despite the nervous tension in the air, there was a sense of calm between us now—like this moment was exactly where I was supposed to be, exactly where we were supposed to be.

I picked up the conversation like nothing had changed, like this was always meant to unfold this way.

CHAPTER EIGHT
PIPER

Ever since Lane and I's trip to Crestview, we spoke more and more. He seemed to be writing more, too. I hadn't outright asked him, but I had a feeling that the trip had sparked some inspiration in him. I know it sparked something in me. Especially when I was alone in bed at night. That kiss... It was electric. I remembered the kisses we shared in high school—passionate, always with that magnetic pull between us. But this... this caught me off guard. It was sweet, simple, and left me with a lingering warmth.

But as the days wore on, I also couldn't ignore the fact that he had hurt me.

It had been a long time, and I knew it was time to let go, to stop holding onto old grudges. But I wasn't sure I could keep going with whatever was unfolding between Lane and me without confronting the past.

Before I could dive into that, though, the holidays hit us full force. Thanksgiving was tomorrow, and I had a ton to do.

The countdown to Small Business Saturday and the Pine Hills Christmas Kickoff were on, and I had to make sure the bookshop was ready. The Saturday after Thanksgiving was the official kickoff to Christmas in Pine Hills, and it was one of the busiest shopping days of the year. The whole town came alive with festivities—parades, a Christmas market, reindeer, carriage rides, and even a brew tent. People traveled from all over to join in on the celebration, and it was up to the city's planning committee to make it unforgettable.

This year was extra special—it was the 75th Christmas Kickoff, so we were pulling out all the stops. Between managing the bookshop and checking in with other businesses, I was running around like crazy. The team was solid, though, and it was reassuring to know they had everything covered at our other stores. After losing my dad and with my mom being sick, I appreciated my staff more than ever.

By the time I was done for the day, it was almost 11 PM. Bennett's Books was ready for the after Thanksgiving shopping. The shop was stocked, the gift-wrapping station was set up, and the decorations were in place. I took a deep breath, turned off the lights, and made my way upstairs.

As I opened my door, it hit me—I didn't have Sasha with me, and I still needed to invite Lane over for Thanksgiving. My grandparents had insisted on stuffing him with food. I'd told them he probably had his own family plans, but they insisted he stop by at least to say hello.

I knocked on Lane's door, and after a moment, it swung open. There he stood. No shirt, muscles on full display, and I was completely dumbstruck. His chest was tight, abs defined, arms massive and strong. I couldn't help but stare, my gaze falling to his collarbones and then to his tan joggers. The happy trail leading down... and that V-cut. I swear, I was salivating.

"Hey, Pipes," he said, his grin teasing as he caught me staring.

I couldn't even get words out—just a mess of incoherent sounds.

"You okay? You need something?" He asked, clearly amused.

"I do. I need to ask you something," I said, my voice slow and breathy. Was I *purring*? Jesus, I sounded like a lovesick woman. I cleared my throat, trying to regain composure. "I need to grab Sasha. She's probably still downstairs. But before I go, I wanted to see if you'd come by my grandparents' for Thanksgiving. I know you probably have your own family plans, but they really want to see you. You can even bring your sister and her family if you want. The more, the merrier."

"Yeah, I was planning on it. I think I'll be there most of the day. Do you want to ride together? I guess your grandma talked to my sister about our plans. She's not much of a cook and was more than happy to accept the invitation. I thought you knew." He was smiling, but was that a pec flex I just saw?

I think I nearly moaned. "Oh, yeah."

"You okay there? You're drooling." Lane's voice broke through my fog. I snapped out of it and quickly wiped my mouth. There was no drool.

"You ass," I said, smiling as I fought to keep it together.

He laughed. "I'll take that as a compliment, since you were basically undressing me with your eyes just now." He chuckled, and it made me realize how much I was enjoying this—how much I was enjoying *him*.

"Anyway," he continued, "Sasha's with me. Let me go wake up my baby girl." He turned and sauntered off into his place, and I couldn't help but watch the way his joggers fit his... well, everything.

Then it hit me. What did he just say? *Was my dog cheating on me with him?*

I followed him into his apartment, still in disbelief. And then I saw Sasha curled up on the couch, snoring softly.

"What is this? What's going on here?" I asked, trying to sound annoyed, though I was fighting a smile.

Lane looked a little embarrassed, like he'd been caught doing something he shouldn't.

"Spill it. What have you and Sasha been up to behind my back, Lane?" I crossed my arms, pretending to be stern. "Tell me now, or I'll uninvite you from Thanksgiving, and Sasha will only get dry dog food tomorrow."

Lane ruffled his hair, clearly trying to hold back laughter. "So, uh, it started a few days after I moved in. She'd come by my door, I'd let her in, we'd cuddle, I'd give her a treat, and then she'd leave after an hour. But lately, with you getting ready for the Christmas rush and me busy writing, she started coming up more often and staying longer. Now she has a spot on the couch, and I even got her a water bowl. I take her for walks every afternoon too. I'm sorry, Piper. I thought you knew by now."

I tried to keep my stern expression, but a smile crept onto my face. My dog had fallen for Lane Schiller. And, truthfully, I was falling for him a little more, too. The dislike was slowly evaporating. Especially after the kiss in Crestview.

"So, what you're telling me is that you and my dog have been hanging out behind my back?"

"In fairness," he said, laughing, "I thought you knew. If Sasha could talk, she would've told you herself. It wasn't supposed to be a secret this long. It started out as a secret between her and I, but then I guess I thought you just caught on."

I shook my head, a laugh escaping my lips. "Well, this is just great. My dog and my frenemy are bonding now. What am I supposed to do with that?"

Lane grinned and his eyes had this ravenous desire in them. "Just let it happen. You can't break our bond now. And I think I have moved past the frenemy stage. Don't you?"

Sasha chose that moment to get up and slowly walk over to me, nudging her head against my hip. My big bear dog had found another human who loved her as much as I did.

I sighed, pretending to still be upset, but I couldn't help the affection I felt. "Alright, I guess you can still come to Thanksgiving, but I'm more upset with Sasha. She might only get gravy on her dry food instead of turkey. Depends on how much she grovels."

Sasha, as if on cue, gave her best sad dog eyes, and Lane grinned. "I'll make sure she grovels. And I'll grovel for her too. She *needs* that slice of turkey. She's the best girl."

I laughed. "Okay, okay. You're both getting turkey. But only because you're both so damn charming."

Lane scratched the top of Sasha's head and turned to me with a smile. "So, what time do we need to be at your grandparents' tomorrow?"

"I'll need to get there by 9 in the morning. I help with the setup. Plus, my grandpa makes the best Bloody Mary, and you can't start Thanksgiving without being a few sheets to the wind."

Lane's grin widened. "Sounds perfect. I'll drive us. I'll meet you in the hallway at 8:45?"

"We don't need to drive," I said, turning back to head to my apartment. "They live a few blocks away. We can walk. That way you can join in on the festivities. But I'll let you be my designated walker after everything is done."

Lane laughed. "Sounds like tomorrow is going to be a blast."

"You know it!" I chimed back, smiling as I shut the door behind me.

CHAPTER NINE
LANE

The day started wonderfully. Getting ready for Thanksgiving with the Bennetts was relaxed, fun, and filled with Bloody Marys. By the time my sister, her husband, and their kids arrived, I was feeling a strong buzz. Mark, my sister's husband, immediately jumped on the Bloody Mary bandwagon. We bonded over it, and for the first time, I saw why my sister loved him so much. I had always viewed him as a prissy doctor who spent his time reading medical journals, but today, he surprised me. He was a cool guy, and I actually enjoyed hanging out with him.

As the day wore on, Piper became increasingly anxious. She was fidgeting and glancing at the clock, as though she was waiting for someone. I could see her grandparents becoming equally uneasy as the clock ticked closer to mealtime. At 1:30, Piper went to the garage to grab a beer, and I knew she needed a moment to herself. But I couldn't resist following her.

When I got to the garage, I found her leaning against her grandparents' car, wiping her eyes. She was crying. My protective instincts kicked in immediately.

"Pipes, is everything okay?" I rushed over and rubbed her arms comfortingly.

"I'm fine. Everything's fine," she said, her voice wavering, as a sob escaped.

"It's not. Is there anything I can do?" I asked, trying to offer support.

"I hate this. I don't want to cry when today has been so great," she muttered, rubbing her eyes.

"It's okay to cry. If you need to talk, I'm here for you." I slung my arm around her shoulders, pulling her close.

"You're being so nice," she sniffled. "But I'm upset for a few reasons. My mom hasn't answered my calls, and she should've arrived by now. I'm guessing she's not coming because this is the first Thanksgiving without my dad." More tears fell as she choked on the last few words.

"Oh, Pipes, I'm so sorry. I should've known this would be tough for you. I didn't even think about it." My heart ached for her. Losing her dad, her grandparents losing their son, and her mom battling cancer—it was all so much to carry.

"I think we should check on your mom. You don't have to do this alone," I suggested, wanting to help somehow.

"I don't know, Lane. My mom's been a shell of herself since Dad died. She thinks she should've been the one to go, not him."

"That's got to be tough for her. But it's hard on you too. I can see how worried you are. Let's go check on her together, bring her some food. I think it'll help." I brushed a tear from her cheek, giving her a soft smile.

"Okay," she whispered in agreement, though it was clear she wasn't completely sure.

We went inside and explained the plan to everyone. They immediately started gathering food, and within fifteen minutes, we were headed to her mom's house. Piper insisted I join, even though I thought it should be a private moment. The determined look in her eyes told me she needed me there for support. I wanted to be there for her. While she was always taking care of everyone else, it was time for me to take care of her.

I realized, as we made our way to her mom's house, that I was falling for Piper harder than I expected. It was both exciting and terrifying. I couldn't bear the thought of this feeling not lasting.

When we arrived at the door, I could see the tension in Piper's body. She squeezed my hand, and I squeezed it back, silently reassuring her I was there.

Her grandmother knocked, then pressed the Ring doorbell. A moment later, Piper's mom opened the door. She looked tired, fragile—nothing like the woman I remembered from a few years ago. It broke my heart to see her like this.

Without hesitation, Mrs. Bennett entered, announcing that she'd brought food. Piper's mom looked confused, almost dazed. Piper walked up to her, wrapping her arms around her shoulders.

"Hi, Mom. I was worried about you. Since you weren't at Grandma and Grandpa's, we wanted to check in." Her mom reached out, gently pulling Piper into a hug. A single tear rolled down her cheek.

"Oh, Pipe. I couldn't do it," her mother sobbed harder.

Piper hugged her back, swaying slightly, her voice soft as she reassured her mother that everything would be okay.

The scene was deeply moving, and I felt like an intruder, unsure if I should stay or leave. But before I could decide, Mrs. Bennett called me into the kitchen, saving me from the awkwardness.

I walked into the kitchen, grateful for the distraction. "How can I help, Mrs. Bennett?" I asked.

"You can help by rinsing those dishes and putting them in the dishwasher," she replied, breaking down a cardboard box. She didn't need to ask me twice—I immediately got to work.

As we cleaned, Mrs. Bennett talked quietly. "You know, Lane,

Mary and my son were the perfect pair. They were so in love. They met in high school, broke up for a bit, and then got back together when they ran into each other here in Pine Hills. Kinda like you and Piper. Losing my son has been hard, but Mary losing her true love—well, that's broken me even more. She feels like she should've been the one to die, not him. But she deserves to survive. She has to. For Piper's sake."

I didn't respond, focusing on rinsing the dishes. Her words weighed heavily on me. In many ways, Piper and I were like her parents—two people who had been through so much, yet found their way back to each other. At least I hope we were finding our way back to one another. I was understanding the depth of that kind of connection.

Just then, Piper and her mother entered the kitchen. Piper was holding her mother's hand, and her eyes were red from crying.

"I appreciate you all coming over," Mary mumbled. "I got so caught up in Travis not being here, and I..." she trailed off with a sob.

Mrs. Bennett rushed over to embrace her. "It's okay, dear. Today's hard for all of us. But being together makes it a little easier. Why don't you come to our place? I think it'll help."

Mary nodded, agreeing. "You're right."

Piper stood there, her eyes glistening, and I could feel the weight of the moment settling over us. It was heartbreaking, but also beautiful, to witness so much love and compassion.

When we returned to Mrs. Bennett's house with Mary, we were met with hugs and a buzz of activity. The mood was filled with eager hunger as everyone readied for the meal. Mrs. Bennett went straight to work, making sure everything was laid out perfectly. Piper set another place at the table for her mother.

I took a seat next to Piper and gently placed my hand on her knee. She looked at me with a mix of surprise and something else

—something I couldn't quite read. I leaned over and whispered in her ear, "Thank you for inviting us. Today has been perfect."

She looked back at me, her expression soft, and in that moment, I knew for sure that I wanted her. I wanted this - the good days and the bad. All of it.

CHAPTER TEN
PIPER

With Christmas just twelve days away, I was swamped with orders. The last few weeks had been a blur, and I'd barely seen Lane. On the other hand, my mom was slowly getting back to her old self. She was working a few hours a week at her flower shop with my aunt and helping me fulfill orders at the bookstore. Her help was much appreciated since Lola and I were running around like mad. It was good for her, too—she was starting to get a sparkle back in her eye.

Getting her out of her slump on Thanksgiving had been exactly what she needed. It showed her there was still more life to live, and once she was back at my grandparents' house, everyone made sure she had fun. They treated her like everything was normal, and I could see how important it was for her to avoid isolation. She needed to focus on the positive and be surrounded by joy and love, not the weight of the past year.

"Piper! Honey! Can you come here, please?" I heard my mom calling from the front counter. She was grabbing books off the shelves to bring to the back so I could send them off.

"Coming!" I called back, walking to the front. As I stepped

through the curtain, I saw Lane standing behind the counter, and my mom was wearing a devious, gigantic smile.

"What's going on? You two look suspicious," I asked, raising an eyebrow.

"Lane stopped by to see if you were busy. I told him you weren't and could use a break from the store." My mom's grin was pure mischief.

"Mom, I'm too busy to take a break. There are too many orders," I protested.

"Piper, come with me. It's only for a few hours. I have something I want to show you," Lane said, his voice coaxing.

"I don't think I have a few 'hours' to spare, Lane. I have a business to run," I replied, but I could already feel the exhaustion creeping in.

"Piper, you're going. End of story. Get out of here." My mom handed me my coat and beanie, giving me a playful swat on the butt. "Go on now."

I didn't want to go, but a break would be nice. "Fine. But if anything becomes an emergency, please, please, call me." I turned back to hug my mom, quickly moving out of the store's front door to join Lane.

As we walked down the street, I felt the weight on my shoulders begin to lift. Maybe a walk would be good, since I'd been so consumed by work lately. We walked in silence for a while, and I noticed all the shop windows with their Christmas decorations. I hadn't stopped to appreciate how cute Pine Hills looked for the holidays. Normally, I'd be swept up in the Christmas spirit, but this year, it felt like the joy was missing. Losing my dad had cast a shadow, and the usual excitement wasn't there.

But as we walked together, I started to feel a small spark of the Christmas magic again. I smiled at the town's decorations, people bustling with kindness, and the familiar sense of community. I looked up at Lane, and my breath caught in my throat. He was so handsome. Then, unexpectedly, he grabbed my hand, and I couldn't help but swoon.

"I was thinking we could hop in my car, and go to a place I've been wanting to take you," Lane said, smirking with that mischievous glint in his eye.

"Are you going to take me somewhere to murder me? Should I be concerned?" I joked, my heart racing a little.

"No, Pipes. You'll love it. I need a break from writing. You need a break from the store. It'll be good for both of us to just relax," he replied, still smiling as we approached his car. I hesitated for a second, but then I hopped in.

After about an hour of driving, we stumbled upon a quaint little town called Englishton. I'd never expected it to be so charming. I always loved getting farther out of Pine Hills and New York City. Distance brought peace—a respite from the chaos of everyday life. When Lane pulled into a parking spot in front of a cute little Italian restaurant, I smiled.

"Well, we're here. This is my favorite Italian place. We used to meet my grandparents here when we were kids. I loved it. I actually based one of my characters on the owner. His demeanor was perfect for an old doctor in one of my books," Lane said, his voice filled with nostalgia as he glanced at the restaurant.

"Are you talking about Doctor McGrundy from *Forever & Ever & Ever*?" I asked with a shy smile. I wasn't sure if he'd be surprised, but I wasn't lying when I said I had read all of his books.

Instead, Lane smiled down at me. "You're giving me the impression of a stalker, Pipes. Maybe I should start locking my door at night."

"You don't lock your door at night?" I asked, baffled.

Lane laughed. "I do now, but you're making me reconsider a deadbolt."

I swatted him for the umpteenth time. *This guy.*

We walked into the restaurant, and the smell of sweet spices and dough immediately hit me. It was the scent of comfort, food, of joy. I knew I was in for a treat. The food was amazing, and the conversation was even better. The wine was flowing, and my one too many glasses of it were superb. This brief break was exactly what I needed. If I could rate the food, company, and restaurant, it would be a ten out of ten.

As we left the restaurant, Lane led me in a different direction, away from the car.

"Where are we going?" I asked, my tipsy brain now more curious than anything.

"We're going to walk around, enjoy the afternoon. We can shop in the stores if we want, get coffee, whatever we feel like," Lane replied, sounding so calm and free.

It hit me then—I needed the calm of today. Everything had been hectic lately, and I hadn't taken a moment to simply be in the present. To breathe.

I hurried to match Lane's stride, and my mind began to wander. I thought about holding his hand. My sober, logical brain said no. But my wine-addled brain shouted, *Yes, girl!*

And so, my give-a-fucks were gone. I reached for his hand. Lane looked down at me and smiled, not saying a word. A wave of rightness washed over me. This was exactly where I was supposed to be.

CHAPTER ELEVEN

LANE

The trip to Englishton was one for the books. The smiles Piper kept flashing me throughout the day got me every time. Spending a relaxed afternoon with her was perfect, and I couldn't stop staring at her. She was back to being carefree, having fun—letting go of the weight of the past year and the constant pressure of work. For a few hours, she had been liberated.

When we returned to the bookstore, Sasha was waiting at the front door, wagging her big Newfie bottom. She wasn't used to being left alone in the shop, and when Piper unlocked the door, Sasha knocked both of us over in excitement. Of course, I had to give my best girl all the pets and love for being such a trooper while we were gone.

"She loves you deeply, you know? I can tell. You've totally won her over," Piper said from the ground, still petting the massive bear-dog with a relaxed smile.

"I love her too. Like it or not, I've formed an intense bond with Sasha, and she's stolen my heart. She might just have to become my dog. Maybe we should get a custody agreement drawn up," I joked.

"Hardy, har, har. You've got such a hilarious sense of humor." Piper took my hand, and I pulled her up. She hopped to her feet, and suddenly her face and body were so close to mine that I could feel the heat of her chest against mine. I inhaled deeply, catching the vanilla and coconut scent of her shampoo.

She placed her hands on my chest, and her voice was soft. "I had the best time with you today. I really needed this."

"I did too, Pipes." I leaned in and kissed her, pouring all my tenderness into that single, delicate moment. Our lips met in a perfect union, a kiss that felt like it could stretch on forever. When we finally broke apart, her eyes were still closed, a soft smile playing on her lips.

"I'm savoring this moment. It's perfect. And it just reminds me I should probably hang some mistletoe in the store." She opened her eyes, still wearing that beautiful smile.

"Your brain goes all over the place," I said, teasing.

"That it does, good sir," she replied with a playful grin.

We closed up the shop, and Piper lingered, taking her time to double-check everything, even though Lola and her mom had already taken care of it all. There was something magnetic about watching her like this—fully in her element, giving attention to the store, the customers, the books. It was a side of her I always admired. When she finally seemed satisfied, we made our way up the stairs to our respective apartments. The space between us felt charged with something electric, and I ached to ask her inside. I wanted to pull her close, to feel the warmth of her against me, to keep the lightness of the day alive. I didn't want this moment to end.

"Thanks again, Lane. Today was really special," she said, unlocking her door. I just stood there like a teenager on his first date, not wanting to move.

"I'm going to hit the hay, but can we get together this weekend? Want to come over for dinner? I'll cook," she asked, and I could hear the slight nervousness in her voice.

I felt a bit deflated, not ready for the night to end. Over the past few weeks, we had been weaving together a new kind of friendship—one that felt more like something deeper. So I said, "I'd like that. But, please, tell me you're not going to make lasagna like you did in high school, are you?" I teased.

She laughed. "Oh, you are such an ass," she said, but I could hear the affection in her voice. "It was pretty bad, though." She paused and then added, "I've since learned how to cook. I promise it won't taste like garbage or leave you sick on the toilet for two days, like last time. I'll let you know what day works. Goodnight, Lane."

She waved and backed into her apartment, Sasha following close behind. The door clicked shut, and I stood in the hallway, wishing I'd asked her to hang out for just a few more minutes.

Three days before Christmas, Piper had caught up on her work and finally asked me to dinner at her place. I'd been nervous she might never ask with everything she had going on. Her mother had been helping her every day, and I had chipped in with the cleaning and restocking. Watching them together made me happy—they seemed to be finding their rhythm again. An early Christmas present arrived, and the news was nothing short of a miracle: Mary's last scan showed no signs of cancer. The joy that filled Piper and her mom was contagious, and I could see the shift in their energy.

I was still nervous, though. I had been writing like mad, pouring all my inspiration into the pages, often with Sasha by my side as my loyal companion. When I wasn't at the shop or writing, I'd spent time with my niece and nephew, and had even begun imagining myself settling down in Pine Hills. The idea of being close to my family and old friends felt right.

But what felt even more real was how things with Piper were unfolding. We were tip-toeing around the past—the heartbreak from high school. I wasn't sure if tonight was the right time to dig into it, but I knew we couldn't avoid it forever. She had broken my heart back then, and though we had been friends for so long, the chemistry between us had grown into something I couldn't ignore anymore.

We had spent our lives knowing all the little details about each other, and as we flirted more, I got eager. I felt confident that my life was finally moving in the right direction. I felt lucky. But then came that moment—when she got the acceptance letter to Columbia, and everything changed. I thought we would both go to NYU. I thought we were on the same path. But we weren't.

Piper was thrilled, of course, and I felt stupid for being upset. She had applied for a scholarship and had earned it. But in the end, I didn't ask her out that day. I needed time to process.

When I finally went to talk to Piper after my track practice, she was livid. Tears filled her eyes, and her face was red with frustration. She paced back and forth in front of my car, and when she spoke, her words cut deep.

"What's the matter, Pipes?" I asked, my heart pounding.

"You know, Lane, I always thought you were the nicest person in my life. You were always there for me, always one of my best friends. And then I fell for you, and I thought you were falling for me. Now, I realize I was an idiot."

"What are you talking about? What's going on?" Panic rushed through me. Her words were coming from left field, and I couldn't understand.

"Avoiding me for a week was one thing, but I thought you would have the decency to tell me what was going on. Instead, I had to find out from Sheera. I wondered why people were laughing at me. Now I know. Now I know you're not the nice guy I thought you were. You're an asshole who uses girls, and when you don't get what you want, you drop them. So fuck you, Lane. I want nothing more to do with you. Go fuck yourself!" She ran away, leaving me standing there, frozen.

I was stunned and just stood in place. When I realized I should pursue her, she had already left. So I didn't chase after her, and by the time I realized what I had done, it was too late.

Thinking back on it makes me ache. I should have gone to her house. I should have called her, done anything. But I didn't. I hung my head, ashamed, and moved on. I spent the summer with friends in the Hamptons, went off to college, and buried the "what ifs."

But no matter how much I tried to forget, I kept writing about her. I kept writing her as the love interest in every book I'd ever written. She was the one that got away.

Now, I was on the brink of getting her back. So close to reclaiming the life I'd always wanted—the life in Pine Hills, near my family, near old friends... and near Piper. But the past had to come up. We couldn't avoid it any longer. I needed answers, needed to understand what happened and why the pieces of my broken heart never seemed to fit back together. Deep down, I knew that Piper was the only one who could mend it.

CHAPTER TWELVE
PIPER

I was moving and shaking, getting everything prepped for dinner. I aimed for a meal that was easy yet wholesome. With my never-ending to-do list for the bookstore and the other shops, cooking something fancy was out of the question. So I opted for Potato Bacon Soup in the crockpot. Simple. Wholesome. Casual. I hoped. And besides, Lane wouldn't be able to make fun of me. It'd be hard to mess this up.

I told Lane to come over for dinner around 6:30 p.m. By 5:45, I still needed to change and freshen up from a day spent working my fanny off. I hopped in the shower to rinse off, brushed my teeth, put on a fresh coat of mascara and eyeliner, then slipped into joggers and a sweatshirt. I told him to dress comfy and casual, since we'd be watching a movie afterward.

To keep it non-romantic and chill, I picked *Die Hard* for our Christmas movie. I'd first watched it with Lane back in our sophomore year of high school, and the nostalgia would be high. Sasha was fed and snoring away on her massive dog bed next to the couch. Gazing at her, I couldn't help but think how being a dog was the best way to live—well loved, fed, watered, and belly rubs all day long.

Since our afternoon at Englishton, my feelings had been at the forefront of my mind. I was falling for Lane ... again. Every time I saw him, my mood lifted. Speaking with him always made me smile. When he grabbed my hand, hugged me, or kissed my forehead, it felt like comfort and love wrapping around me. I felt safe. But the moment I was alone, the past came rushing back—the way he had shattered me at the end of senior year. We couldn't avoid it much longer. We needed to face it. My heart couldn't keep falling for a man who'd once left it in pieces. I didn't think I could put it back together again a second time.

Lane arrived right at 6:30, and I let him in with an overly dramatic arm swing, as if to showcase my humble loft. "Welcome to my humble abode, Sir Lane. This is where we'll dine tonight and watch our feature film."

I gestured for him to follow me into the rest of the space. My loft was a lot like his, but with floor-to-ceiling windows that faced the main street of Pine Hills. The open layout ran the length of the room, letting in so much light. My apartment had a bedroom, a second room that doubled as a bedroom and library, and one and a half bathrooms.

"Wow! This is a really cool place, Piper. It fits you." Lane looked around in awe. Despite the bare brick-and-concrete space with exposed pipes, I'd worked hard to make it feel cozy. There were plants everywhere, comfy couches, and a big reading chair by one of the windows. Various rugs covered the floor, warming up the place. On the walls were art, shelves of books, plants, and framed photos of family, friends, and Sasha.

"Thanks, Lane. I've worked hard to make it cozy. When I first moved in, it was cold and loud. I could hear a pin drop. But now? It's my safe space, and I relax the second I step through the door."

"That's awesome. I'm hoping to find a place that gives me that feeling soon. I don't have that at my apartment in New York. Hell, my furniture's white, and it's not even mine. It came with the place."

"Wow. You really are a typical New Yorker, huh?" I teased.

"Yup. But hopefully, not for much longer." He gave me a look —a mix of longing, hope, and a hint of something like apprehension.

"I sense you have something you want to tell me?" I asked, my tone playful but also curious. No sense in beating around the bush with Lane. I'd been open with him, and I felt comfortable asking.

"There's something I do want to talk about. But let's eat and catch up first." He went to sit at the island counter.

"That works for me. Are you in the mood for wine or beer?"

"Beer's good." He grinned. "So, how was your day, Piper? Tell me everything."

I smiled and slid the beer across to him. "It was great. Last-minute shoppers packed the store, and I know it'll get even busier since Christmas is only a few days away. We're closing at noon on Christmas Eve for the first time this year. Usually, we stay open until 6, but I wanted to give Lola a chance to prep for Christmas. I also took Sasha on two long walks and played fetch with her in the snow. She's not great at fetch since she's so big, but it's fun to watch. Oh, and I started writing a book this week. I forgot to ask, do you like Potato Bacon Soup? That's what we're having."

I realized I was rambling and quickly flushed with nerves. I had over-talked.

Lane took it all in stride, though, giving me a reassuring smile. "Wow! Sounds busy! And I love soup—it's been making the entire upstairs smell amazing today. I was wondering what you were cooking. But can we go back to this 'writing a book' thing? You kind of dropped it on me."

"Uh, yeah. We can get back to that, I guess. I mean... I've always wanted to write, you know that. I went to school for it, and

I should've been writing all along. I've had a few ideas over the years, but something sparked recently, and now I'm writing every day. So yeah, it's happening."

I was blushing, embarrassed. Here I was, telling one of my favorite authors—and potential love interest—that I was trying to be like him, a writer.

"Piper," Lane stood up from his stool and came around the island to hug me. "That's fucking awesome. You wrote the best stories growing up. Honestly, you kind of inspired me. I don't think I'd be half the writer I am today without you. I'm proud of you."

I melted. Hearing the words "I'm proud of you" and knowing I'd inspired him was like chocolate fondue—sweet and warm.

"Thanks, Lane. Coming from you, the 'oh-so-glorious New York Times Bestselling Author,' that means a lot." I gazed up at him, suddenly feeling emotional. "I don't know why I'm getting so choked up about it, but I am."

"I mean it. You've got so much talent. Please, keep writing. It's your dream." He hugged me again, and I melted into the comfort of his embrace. His powerful arms, his firm body ... I felt safe, held, like I belonged right there with him.

I wasn't great at showing vulnerability, but with Lane, it felt easy. I whispered, "It's so nice being in your arms."

Lane didn't let go. Instead, he swayed us together and said, "It's perfect."

And just like that, I was done. I had fallen—fallen in love with Lane. Again. And I didn't want this to end. So we stayed like that, swaying to the background music I had forgotten was playing. After a few minutes, Lane's stomach growled, breaking the spell.

"It's time to eat, yeah?"

"Yep. It sure is."

I scooped out spoonfuls of potato soup into large bowls for me and Lane, placing oyster crackers and saltines on the table in case he wanted an extra crunch. I usually added oyster crackers to mine, and we sat down to talk about life. Lane told me about his writing days and how much he loved Pine Hills. He mentioned hanging out with his niece and nephew, how his sister and brother-in-law were happy to have him around. He also shared that his parents were flying in the day after Christmas to visit. It was nice—casual, comforting conversation.

Once we finished dinner, we moved to the couch, and I started the movie.

"*Die Hard*? Really, Piper?" Lane chuckled, shaking his head. "Do you remember when I made you watch this at your parent's house in, what, 11th grade? You hated it! You made me watch *Love Actually* afterward just to make up for it."

Laughing, I replied, "I do. Hence, the reason I picked it."

"You never stop surprising me, or mesmerizing me, Piper."

His words caught me off guard, and I glanced at him. He was looking at me with such intense longing in his eyes and reached over to move a stray piece of hair off my cheek. My blush betrayed my uncertainty about where this was headed. But before I could stop myself, I blurted, "I do?"

"You do. You always have."

Silence filled the space, stretching uncomfortably until Lane broke it again. "Piper. We need to discuss the past. And we need to discuss the future. As much as I want to watch *Die Hard* with you, I need to have this conversation."

My stomach flipped. I'd known this was coming. We had to hash it out before things went any further.

"Sure, Lane. Let's talk." I exhaled deeply, bracing myself. "You didn't apologize. You didn't explain why you did what you did. Instead, you moved on and left me alone. And it hurt. It broke me, Lane. I spent the entire summer with Bri and Sam, picking up the pieces after losing you. I was falling for you—madly, deeply in love with you—and you were one of my best friends. Then, one minute we were hanging out, making out, holding hands. I was sure you were going to ask me to be your girlfriend. The next thing I know, you're talking to Sheera. I heard you were taking her to prom because 'she vibed with you better,' and that it didn't look good for the prom king and queen to go with other people. Then I was told you were 'keeping your options open,' and I was just some fool for pining for you. The worst part? The rumors that you were making fun of me. Then, when I yelled at you, you said nothing. No explanation. No apology. You just... let it go. And that hurt even more. After years of being best friends, you didn't even try to fight for our friendship."

I took a deep breath, exhaling slowly. Saying it out loud felt strangely liberating. Before Lane could speak, I added, "I want you to know that when you walked into my bookstore, I still had so much anger toward you. It brought back all those feelings of insecurity, loss, and brokenness... I wasn't nice to you at first, and I'm sorry. But over the past month, my feelings have changed. Lane, I'm falling for you again, and it's terrifying. I don't want anyone to hurt me again, especially you. You can't break my heart a second time. Please don't."

Tears streamed down my face as I hugged my knees to my chest. Lane scooted closer and took my hands in his.

"Piper, I don't want to hurt you. Doing that is the last thing I'd ever want. I don't want to get hurt again, either." He paused, and I looked at him, surprised. "Can I tell you my side? Can I tell you how I feel?"

I nodded, squeezing his hands. "Of course. Please, share."

"Your story is different from mine. That's the beauty of differing perspectives." He smiled faintly. "So, here's mine, Piper Ann Bennett. Once upon a time, I met a girl with no bottom front teeth who was scraping an apple with her top front teeth. I thought she was a weirdo. She told me she was toughening her teeth like a beaver with wood. I laughed and told her she was a dork. She smiled and said I was one too—and since our parents were friends, we should be friends too."

I smiled at the memory, hearing him talk about the first time we met, when we were five.

"Over the years, we became best friends, and she knew all my secrets—my ugly habits, my flaws. She knew my favorite song, my favorite book, and even my favorite pair of underwear."

"Oh my gosh, I forgot about your Beavis and Butt-Head underwear!" I laughed.

He grinned. "Yeah, well, we were sophomores when I made her watch *Die Hard* as a joke. But that was the first time we hung out just the two of us, no parents or friends. Little did she know, I'd been crushing on her since I was ten, and I thought, 'Tonight's the night. I'm going to tell her how I feel.' But it didn't go that way, as you know." He smirked.

"I started flirting with her more after that. Had a few girl-friends, but no one compared to her. I got jealous of her boyfriends." He looked at me, and I swatted him playfully. "Then senior year, it felt like everything was aligning in our favor. Time was whispering, 'Now's the moment.' But I was too nervous to ask her out."

He paused, his face growing more serious. "When I finally got up the nerve, I went to ask her. But she was in her room, staring at a piece of paper, jumping up and down and screaming. I knew it was her NYU acceptance letter. That was when it hit me: she had a future planned without me in it. She hadn't even told me she'd applied to Columbia. I pretended to be happy for her, but deep down, I was torn. The girl I loved, who had been my best friend for years, was going off without me."

I stopped holding my knees and crossed my legs, grabbing Lane's hands. His eyes were wet as he spoke, and I felt my heart ache for him.

"Lane, I... I didn't know. I'm so sorry. I didn't even tell my parents about Columbia. Not a soul. I didn't want anyone to know."

He wiped his eyes, his voice thick. "It hurt. And instead of talking to you, I took a break to sort things out. But that break led to all kinds of misunderstandings. I never planned to take Sheera to prom. That week, I hung out with Lucas and Everett, went to a few parties, and talked to my parents about you. I only spoke to Sheera at one party, and I told her I was going with you."

My mouth fell open in surprise, and I immediately got angry. "That explains everything. Sheera must have spread those rumors to hurt me. She always had a thing for you."

Lane's eyes narrowed. "Believe me, I know. She stalked me after I took her to prom. I couldn't get away from her until I went to the Hamptons for the summer." He sighed. "Anyway, back to my story..."

"Please," I urged softly, holding his hand and looking into his eyes.

He ran a hand through his hair and seemed lost in the memory. "I remember clearly the day you yelled at me. I meant to apologize for acting so weird. I wanted to ask if I could take you to prom, and maybe, finally ask you to be my girlfriend. But you came up to me, and the way you yelled left me stunned. By the time I thought to chase after you, you were gone. And I was a dumbass. A dumb 18-year-old who drowned his heartbreak in summer parties."

I scooted closer, placing my hands on his knee. "We were kids, Lane. We were both so stupid. I'm sorry. I should have given you a chance to explain when I yelled at you. Maybe we could've avoided all this distance."

"Maybe it was for the best. We lived our lives, and now here we are," he said softly. "I just had dinner with you. I get to kiss you, hold you, and hopefully, I'll convince you to give me a second chance."

His words made my heart swell with hope.

Lane cleared his throat and looked at me with such intensity. "Piper, I want you to understand something. You were always with me. You were the girl I compared every other love interest to. I've always carried this love for you. Always."

He pulled my face toward him and kissed me deeply. Tears streamed down my cheeks as I held onto him, climbing into his lap.

We broke apart for a moment, and I whispered, "I've always loved you too. I love you now."

At that moment, Sasha decided it was the perfect time to wedge her giant head between us. We both laughed and pulled apart, still holding each other.

"I love Sasha too. Almost more than I love you," Lane teased.

I laughed, shaking my head. "Lane, did you really write me into your stories? Was I your muse?"

Lane took my hand and kissed it, then looked deep into my eyes. "Yes, Pipes. All my love interests, all my love stories, they're all because of you."

I wrapped my arms around him, sobbing, a mix of sadness for the lost time and gratitude for where we were now. Maybe all the pain, all the waiting, had been necessary to bring us to this moment.

"So, Piper," Lane asked softly, "can we talk about our future now?"

I smiled and wiped my tears. "How about we watch *Die Hard* first? Let me savor this moment for a little longer."

He looked down at me, and I knew we weren't going to be watching the movie. Instead, I reached down and stood up, pulling him toward my bedroom.

"Piper, are you sure? We should talk more. We can take things slow..."

I paused in the hallway and turned to face him. "Come to my bed, please. Let's make the most of the time we've missed."

I tried to be playful, slowly shrugging off my joggers and stepping out of them, pulling my sweater over my head. I was glad I'd worn something sexy underneath my comfy clothes.

"Wow, you're gorgeous."

His eyes roamed over me, and I knew what he said was true. I smirked and motioned for him to follow me. Like a hungry puppy, he did.

CHAPTER THIRTEEN
LANE

It was Christmas Day, and all was silent except for Sasha's snores. Since Piper and I had told each other we loved each other, we hadn't slept apart. After work, I'd go to her place, and we'd sleep there. It felt natural for us. Piper was exhausted and catching up on all the missed "zzz's." Realizing I needed to keep this going, I wasn't tired. I wanted nothing more than to stay in bed with her for days, just watching her sleep. I didn't want to sleep in my bed alone. I craved her company forever.

But the world had other plans. I carefully pulled my arm from Piper's head and eased myself off the bed. Sasha lifted her giant head to look at me. I knew that if she moved off the bed, Piper would wake up, but I also knew that Sasha needed to go outside. So, I pulled on my joggers, a sweatshirt, and shoes. I whispered to Sasha, "Come on, let's go potty." And, of course, the beautiful beast jumbled the bed as she climbed off.

Piper poked her head up so fast from her pillow, and before she could say anything, I moved to her side of the bed. "Go back to bed, Pipes. I'm taking Sasha outside." I kissed her forehead and went out to grab Sasha's leash.

. . .

We were walking around a park a block from Piper's. I couldn't stop thinking about how I didn't want this to end. I finally felt like not being in the city had lifted a weight off my shoulders. My Christmas gift to myself was that I'd finished my novel. Stuck in a writing rut, Piper came through again, inspiring me with a story I desperately needed to tell.

As I was walking back, my phone rang. I didn't check who was calling because I knew it was either my parents wishing me a Merry Christmas or my sister asking when Piper and I would open presents.

"Merry Christmas!" I said into the phone.

"Lane! Merry Christmas and a merry one it is!" My editor, LeAnn, was on the line.

"Merry Christmas, LeAnn! How are you today?" I knew she had news, and I was hoping it wasn't anything negative about my new manuscript. But she sounded chipper.

"I'm fantastic. Lane, I loved this novel you sent me. I cried, I laughed. I love dogs so much. This is the book we were hoping to get out of you. We wanted something a little lighter—something that would knock the knickers off all your fans. You hit the nail on the head."

"Wow! Thanks! I'm so glad you liked it," I said, dumbfounded.

"I didn't just like it. I loooooooved it, Lane. When are you planning to return to the city? We've got a lot to discuss, and my boss and the marketing team want to meet you as soon as possible. Is Tuesday okay to meet? That works for everyone."

"Uh, Tuesday? Like, in four days from now?"

"Yes, Lane. That Tuesday. Does that work for you? I figured you'd be dying to come back home. And what about that girl you were seeing? Corinne? Borinne? Morinne?"

I froze. Maureen and I had only gone on a few dates. "I'm with someone new now. Her name is Piper, and she lives here in Pine Hills. I'm not sure I can make it Tuesday. Could we Zoom in instead?"

"Lane, we want to make this big. This is what all the women in the world are looking for in a romance novel. It's cute, it's fun, it's heated, and it has a dog. You checked all the boxes." I could hear her gulping down whatever she was drinking.

"Okay, I'll head to the city for the day. Can we get everything done on Tuesday?"

"Yes! We can do everything on Tuesday. See you then! Have the best day!"

She hung up before I could even say goodbye, leaving me with a knot in my stomach. LeAnn had mentioned Maureen, and honestly, I didn't think I'd go back to the city. This place brought me joy, and I wanted to put down roots here with Piper.

Despite only having been on a few dates with Maureen, she'd been texting me intermittently while I was here. I had told her before I left that I needed to disappear and write. Now, I had to tell her that I wasn't coming back and that I had feelings for someone else. I knew she had been left with hope that I would return and we could start something more solid. I shouldn't have led her on, and I felt horrible.

As I got back to the shop and walked up the stairs, I opened Piper's door to let Sasha in. I should have gone into Piper's place to see if she was still sleeping, maybe start the coffee. But the weight I'd lifted earlier returned, pressing down on me again. Carefully, I closed her door and went into my room. I looked around and realized I didn't belong in this space. I belonged in Piper's space, in her orbit.

I went to my desk—one Piper had picked out for me. It was sturdy, and I had a strong attachment to it. My excitement for the day had dissipated. I had been looking forward to having a relaxing day with Piper and our families, but now, a storm cloud darkened my mood. I needed to fix it.

I took out my phone and texted Maureen. She didn't celebrate Christmas, so I didn't feel so bad texting her. She was likely working on some cases, regardless.

Lane: Hey Maureen, are you able to chat?

Maureen: Yup, XOXO

I called her, and it only rang once before she picked up.

"Hey, Lane! I was hoping I'd hear from you. When will you be back in the city? I want to see you."

"I'll be back on Tuesday."

"That's great! We should get dinner! Maybe we could do takeout and watch a movie at your place? I might be able to shift some work Tuesday night."

She was getting excited. I knew I was about to hurt her feelings, and I probably shouldn't do this now. But honesty was the best policy. And because I was in love with Piper, Maureen needed to know I wasn't fair game.

"Um, well, here's the thing. I told you I didn't want to date anyone. But I wanted you to know that I've fallen for someone else. I just wanted to give you a heads-up. I didn't want you to get the wrong idea if you saw me in the city. Maureen, I'm so sorry."

"Oh. Your call is surprising. Lane, it's Christmas, for fuck's sake! What the hell? Who calls someone on Christmas and lets them know this shit?" She screamed.

"I understand. Again, I'm sorry. But I knew you didn't celebrate, and you'd probably be working, so I didn't think the day mattered. Listen, I can't apologize enough. I wasn't looking for love, but then the love of my life reappeared, and I had to make this work. I'm sorry."

"Just because I don't celebrate doesn't mean I don't still value the fucking holiday! Lane, I genuinely thought you'd vanish, then come back, and we could start dating and build a future together. I feel so dumb. I thought you liked me."

"I know. I'm so sorry. You're wonderful—smart, beautiful—but I love this girl. Always have, and I know I always will."

"Well, isn't that just so noteworthy for you? What an exceptional Christmas for you." Maureen was pissed, but I could hear the hurt in her voice.

"Maureen, you'll find someone as amazing as you. Someone who thinks you run the world and would be glad just to be in your presence." I was trying to be as kind as I could.

"Oh, fuck off, Lane. You and your writer bullshit. I know I'll find someone. I'm a fucking gorgeous and intelligent corporate attorney, and I know my worth. I can and will do better than you." She said, sounding like her normal self.

"You sure can do better than me."

"Damn straight. Have a pleasant life, Lane." And she hung up.

That conversation could've gone much worse, but I still felt horrible. The pressure on my chest eased a little. I put my phone down and rubbed my face with my hands. Then I heard a sniffle. I turned and saw Piper standing there, tears in her eyes.

"Pipes! Why are you crying? Are you okay?" I rushed to her, genuinely concerned. She looked devastated.

"Lane, you had a girlfriend this whole time? Who are you? I can't believe this." She turned so fast, hauling ass out of my place. I heard her door slam shut. By the time I chased her to her door, she had locked it.

"Go away, Lane. You're a fucking liar!" She screamed through the door. I could hear her sobbing, then kicking and hitting the door.

"Piper, open up! It's not what you think. Maureen wasn't my girlfriend." I knocked harder. "Piper, please. Open up!" I knocked again, jiggling the doorknob. "Pipes. Open the door and talk to me. I won't let this happen again like last time. This is a misunderstanding. Open up!"

Nothing.

I stood there for several minutes, hoping she would open the door. But she didn't. Her phone rang and buzzed repeatedly from my calls and texts. I could hear her phone ring, then go silent so fast. I knew she was ignoring me.

After about an hour of unsuccessful attempts to get through to her, I realized I was getting nowhere. I just had to give her time to cool off.

Crushing pain filled my heart. This time, I knew I needed to do things differently than I had in high school. Fighting for her was a necessity, and fight I would. After an hour of sitting in my rented space, I sent a quick message to my sister, telling her I would arrive later because I had some things to handle. I knew the kids were getting antsy, but this was more important. Piper was the love of my life.

I then called Piper's grandma.

"Lane, dear! What can I do for you? Won't I be seeing you this afternoon?" Her voice was warm, but it only made my chest ache more.

My words caught in my throat, and all I could manage was a choked sob before I finally said, "There was a misunderstanding. Piper thinks I had a girlfriend." I swallowed hard, fighting back more tears. "She thinks I don't love her. I can't lose her again like I did in high school. I just need to talk to her. Can you help me?"

"Oh, honey. I'll be right there." She responded quickly, her tone sincere and full of reassurance. I knew she would come through for me.

About twenty minutes later, I heard a knock on the door. I opened it to find Piper's grandparents and her mother standing there.

"What are all of you doing here?" I asked, surprised. "I just need someone to tell Piper to talk to me. I have to fix this."

"Shhh." Piper's grandma stepped in and gently took my arm, guiding me back inside. "Let's get you settled first. You sounded so distraught on the phone. I also brought Gramps here to look after you. We've got coffee and a breakfast sandwich, too."

I just stared down at the floor, unable to focus on anything but the mess I'd created. My elbows were on my knees, hands running through my hair. "I just need to explain."

I finally lifted my gaze to meet theirs. I needed to explain my side to them before they went to Piper. I knew I sounded frantic, but I had to make them understand. "Piper came in and overheard my conversation with this girl, Maureen. My editor called and asked me if I was still seeing her, and I completely forgot about her. I told Maureen I wasn't interested in dating anyone and that I was staying here for a while. We'd exchanged a few texts, just casual 'How's it going?' stuff. I told her I had fallen in love with Piper, and when I went back to the city on Tuesday, I didn't want Maureen to get the wrong idea. We were never in a relationship. We went on a few dates, but that's it. I swear—I told her before I left that I wasn't looking to date."

I realized I was rambling, but I couldn't stop. This was a disaster, and panic was rising in my chest. I stood up, starting to pace in front of the windows.

Piper's grandpa walked over and gently placed his arm around my shoulder. "Lane, it sounds like a simple miscommunication. Let these ladies go see Piper. We'll get you fed and some coffee. How about we watch *Die Hard*?"

I glanced from him to the rest of them, then nodded. "Okay."

Before Piper's grandma and mom left, her grandmother turned to me and added, "Oh, I texted your sister and told her you'd be a bit. I explained what happened, and she said to handle it before coming over. We'll get this sorted out, my dear. Don't worry."

I watched them leave; the door clicking shut behind them. I wanted to believe her, but the knot in my stomach wouldn't loosen. I could only hope she was right.

CHAPTER FOURTEEN
PIPER

My heart ached with an intensity I hadn't known in years. How could I have been so foolish? I had trusted Lane, only to be hurt again. He had swooped in and shattered my heart like it was a fragile ornament, something I had foolishly let my guard down for a second time. I was a mess, utterly broken.

I lay on my bed, wishing the pillow next to me didn't still carry the scent of him. Sasha, sensing my sadness, came to comfort me. She curled up beside me, resting her head on my side and licking me every few minutes, as though she, too, could sense the heartbreak. The poor thing was grieving, too. Lane had become such an ingrained part of our lives.

Everything I had heard coming out of his mouth made it sound like he was breaking up with some girl, and I was the other woman. I felt like all the old wounds from high school—those painful memories and betrayals—had rushed back. My heart ached in ways I didn't know if it could ever recover from. I was falling for him again. And this time, I should have known better. I had been a fool to give Lane Schiller a second chance. He should have never gotten one.

I don't know how long I lay there, crying and cuddling Sasha, but eventually, I heard a knock. I knew it was probably Lane, and I couldn't bring myself to face him. Sasha, sensing something was up, jumped up and ran toward the door, her movements like a miniature pony's canter. My face was puffy, my eyes swollen from crying. I hesitated before following her. I was on the verge of yelling at Lane to leave when I heard my grandmother's voice telling me through the door to invite her in.

Relieved, I swung the door open, surprised to see not just my grandmother, but also my mother standing there. The two of them stepped in and embraced me tightly. Being wrapped in their love was exactly what I needed.

After a long moment of holding me, we moved to the couch.

"Honey, everything is going to be okay," my mother said gently. "Lane told us to come by and check on you."

"Lane told you to come?" I sniffled, still in disbelief.

"He did. Now, spill. Why are you so upset?" My grandmother's voice was sharp, but caring.

I broke down, sobbing loudly as I told them everything. From the heartbreak in high school to how Lane had come back into my life, how I had fallen for him again. The final blow had been realizing that while we were starting something together, he was also involved with someone else. I explained how we had confessed our love for each other, how he'd written me into his stories, and now, I felt like it had all been a scheme to make me fall for him.

After listening to me, my grandmother laughed, throwing her head back in disbelief. "You dummy. You've got it all wrong. Don't you think so, Mary?" She l99ooked at my mom.

"She sure does," my mother agreed with a smile, then leaned

in to gently caress my hair. "Piper Ann, Lane was simply telling a girl who wanted to date him that he was off the market. He had gone on a few dates with her, but before he left, he made it clear he wasn't interested in dating. Then you came along and broke down those walls."

My grandmother had placed a hand on my knee, comforting me with her presence.

"Honey," my mother continued softly, "Lane is just as heartbroken as you are. This is all a misunderstanding. He's worried about you. I think you need to talk to him."

I couldn't believe it. It was Christmas, and I still couldn't fathom that Lane would tell another girl on Christmas that he wasn't interested in her unless they were already in a relationship. Surely she had called, wanting to talk, and like the jerk he was, Lane had broken things off with her instead. The thought of it made me angry, and realizing how easily my family had been convinced that it was all just a misunderstanding made me livid.

"Mom. Grandma. I appreciate you coming over to cheer me up, but it's Christmas. Lane has fooled you. He lied," I snapped.

"No, he didn't, Piper. He loves you," my grandmother said firmly. "We all know it, and we can see it."

"I just don't believe him," I said, frustration bubbling up. "You know what? I need some time alone. I'll come over later for dinner, but I want to be by myself for now."

The two women exchanged a look, some silent conversation passing between them. Then, they stood, eyeing me with a mix of concern and determination.

"Piper, you need to talk to Lane. You've jumped to conclusions without giving him a chance to explain himself," my grandmother said, her tone sharper than I'd ever heard it. "You walked in, heard what you wanted to hear, and that was it. You tend to do that, and I don't want you to lose out on love because you're too damn stubborn."

I gaped at her, stunned. My mother, equally silent, seemed to be taken aback by her forcefulness.

"Give it a few more minutes, then go talk to him, sweetie. Go in with your ears and heart wide open," my mother added, gently cupping my cheek before walking out.

My grandmother placed a hand on my shoulder. "Take it from a woman who's had to deal with your grandfather and a lot of miscommunication for 45 years. Go in and give him some grace. Listen, be respectful, and let him speak his peace. You'll be glad you did."

She followed my mom out the door, and I stood there, watching them walk to Lane's door. Then, I pressed my door shut.

Was I being closed off? Was I too quick to jump to the worst conclusion instead of giving him a chance? If I was being honest with myself, I knew I was. A decade-long misunderstanding had made me unwilling to listen to him. It had fueled the anger and resentment I still carried toward him. Even though we both knew it was ridiculous, neither of us had ever talked about it. And maybe—just maybe—I hadn't let go of all that anger.

I loved him. I had fallen for him, again. But deep down, I was still holding onto that ember of hatred, the feeling that something would go wrong, that the other shoe would drop.

And now, I knew I needed to talk to him. But was I ready?

CHAPTER FIFTEEN

PIPER

Christmas ended up being okay. I finally showered and changed out of my sweats into some fresh ones, then made my way to my grandmother's. Lane and his family never showed up. I hadn't gone to talk to him, because I needed time to process everything. I knew I'd been dramatic, but I also needed space to work through my emotions. We'd fallen pretty fast. It had only been a month, and we weren't officially together. I realized I had to give myself a little grace.

Lane had texted me to say, "Merry Christmas," and I responded with a simple, "You too." That was all I could muster. The anger was slowly fading, but confusion and embarrassment lingered.

A few days later, I woke up early to head down to the shop. I wanted to put away some of the smaller Christmas decorations. The big tree and main decorations stayed until after New Year's, but I liked getting as much as I could packed away. When I opened my door, I was startled to see Lane, also heading out of his apartment.

He was standing there, duffle bag in hand, and we both froze. My heart dropped into my stomach. Was he leaving?

"Oh—uh—hey, Piper," he said, his voice awkward. He looked down the hallway and ran a hand through his hair.

"Are you leaving?" I blurted out, the words spilling out in a panic. I couldn't help myself.

"Yeah, just for a bit," he replied. "I need to work in the city today. I'll be back, though."

My heart did a weird flip. On the one hand, I was relieved he was coming back. On the other, I felt sad that he was leaving and I hadn't even known about it until now. Even though we hadn't spoken since I had freaked out, I had found some comfort in knowing he was just across the hall. I had been planning on talking to him today, but now I wasn't sure what to do.

I realized I had been staring at him for too long, so he spoke up. "Well, I better hit the road. It's supposed to snow later, and I don't want to deal with traffic and bad roads."

"Oh, yeah. Right," I said, my voice thick with nerves. "You said you'd be back, though... When will you be back?" I could feel the anxiety building in my chest, hoping he wouldn't be gone too long.

"I'm hoping to be back tomorrow night, but definitely before the weekend. Can I walk with you downstairs?" He gestured toward the stairs, and we walked side by side, the silence between us heavy.

As we neared the shop, another tenant passed us in the hallway and waved at me, cutting our path off briefly. We both fell silent again, the tension thick as we reached the door to the shop.

"Lane, I—um—I know we need to talk," I said, my voice quiet but determined. "I really need to talk to you. I know I was being irrational and overreacting, but I just needed some time to reflect. Can you make sure you come back? I need to see you."

I was twisting my hands nervously, unable to hide the worry in my eyes.

Lane gave me a soft, reassuring look. "Piper, I know we need to talk too. Please don't worry. I'm just going to work on my new book and complete some details. I'd come back tonight if I could, but with my editor, that's not likely. My goal is to be home tomorrow."

He paused, and we both noticed how he had referred to this place as "home." It was a simple slip, but it spoke volumes.

"I just—" I didn't know how to finish. Thankfully, Sasha, who had been waiting patiently for attention, "ruffed" loudly, interrupting the moment. Lane bent down to scratch her, rubbing her face and cooing at her.

It was a small, sweet moment, and I felt a rush of love seeing Lane interact with Sasha. It was clear how much he cared for her.

When he rose to his feet, he reached for me. With one hand, he cupped the back of my neck, and with the other, he gently held my waist. "Piper," he said softly, "I'll be back. We'll talk. But don't worry. I'm not going anywhere."

Then, he pulled something from his pocket and handed me a letter. "I wrote this the day after Christmas. I was going to leave it on your desk, but now seems like the right time." He gave me the letter, his fingers brushing against mine before he spoke again. "I meant it when I called this place 'home.'"

He kissed the top of my head, and then, without another word or a glance back, he picked up his duffle bag, unlocked the front door, and left.

Tears immediately filled my eyes. I stood there for a moment, the weight of everything crashing down on me, before retreating back to my office. I placed the letter on my desk and stared at it, frozen. I didn't know if I could handle reading it yet. If it held any more hurtful words, I wasn't sure I could bear it.

I decided to work instead, hoping to push the emotions aside for a while.

A few hours later, Lola came up to me. "Piper, I'm sorry to bother you, and it might not be my place, but you seem really down. Maybe you should take a break? You look a little blotchy. I can handle the store."

I stared at her for a moment, my mind still foggy with emotion. But I nodded. She was right. I needed a break. I headed back to my office, the letter still sitting on my desk, taunting me. I took a deep breath and finally opened it, my fingers trembling as I unfolded the paper.

Dear Piper,

By now I am probably off to New York. The reason I'm writing this letter is to tell you I'm not leaving you. I am coming back. I needed to collaborate with my editor on some work. She was enthusiastic about my new book and eager to start working on it immediately. She believes it will be the next big hit. I happen to agree with her.

The book, you see, is once again an ode to you. You have always been my muse. You show up in every novel I have written. I did not fabricate that. For a long time, I believed you were the one who got away. The one who broke my heart, and that was it. Nothing more. However, during the last month, I've learned that's not accurate. You and I had our second chance at love and I don't want to lose out on it. This Christmas season was the start of our second chance at love.

My life has felt monotonous and repetitive for years. My life was incomplete until you returned. You brought light into my life, and I don't want to return to the darkness. I understand now that I was a source of light for you as well. When I first saw you at Bennett's, you were a shell of a person, but in the past month, you've become radiant, brighter than the Christmas tree in Pine Hills Square. You are glowing and regal. You are beautiful. And I know it is because you love me, too.

This second chance rekindled our spirits.

When I get back, I hope we can talk. I will not let you go again. You can count on me to fight for you. I will fight forever if I have to. Give me a third chance, Piper. I promise that our third chance at love will be perfect. The third time's the charm, right?

I've loved you since we were young, and I will love you forever.

-Lane

CHAPTER SIXTEEN
LANE

Leaving Piper was harder than I thought it would be. I had hoped to sneak out quietly, but maybe it was for the best that we crossed paths before I left town. I had written her a letter, one that expressed all the love I had for her, knowing full well that leaving, even for a night, wasn't ideal. It might cause even more strain on an already complicated situation. But clearly, fate had other plans. I hadn't expected to see her, but I was grateful for the brief moment we shared before I left. I only hoped the distance would give her the space to think—and to finally be ready to talk, to clear up all the misunderstandings.

As I made my way to the city, I stopped by my apartment first. I needed to change clothes and check on things. Turning the knob, I braced myself for the emptiness that awaited me inside. It wasn't my home anymore, and it hadn't really ever felt like it. I was done with it. I grabbed what I needed quickly, then made my way to the lobby. I sent an email to my friend who owned the apartment, asking about breaking my lease. A sense of relief washed over me. It was time to move on.

By the time I was at the office, working with my editor and the marketing team, I was excited about going back to Pine Hills. I couldn't wait to tell Piper about the book—essentially a love letter to her—that I was sure would be a hit.

"This is what all women want," LeAnn said in her usual authoritative tone. "You're going to make all the panties drop with this one, Lane."

LeAnn was a natural leader, and if I could get her on board with my new romance novel, I knew I'd win over not just my current fans, but a whole new crowd.

I wanted to text Piper, but there were things to handle on social media. Most of my readers didn't know what I looked like. I kept my identity a mystery, only letting them hear my voice through the male characters I brought to life in my books. It worked for me—my anonymity seemed to help sales, and I liked that so many women assumed a woman was behind the words.

After hours of work, I finally went back to my apartment. I called in an order from my favorite Thai place, picked it up, and walked back to my building. As I grabbed my mail, I felt the familiar weight of loneliness. I missed both Piper and Pine Hills— the comfort of my family, the little loft above Bennett's. I longed for Sasha, and the stale, empty apartment I returned to felt like a hollow shell.

Tonight, I told myself, was all that mattered. LeAnn and I had debated over working more this week, but I'd put my foot down. She worked her magic, and we got everything wrapped up, with plans to address the rest after New Year's. I was motivated to get back to Pine Hills and start my new life.

Then, my phone dinged. I assumed it was LeAnn, but when I saw Piper's name on the screen, my heart skipped a beat.

Piper: *Hey. How was your day?*

. . .

Lane: *Busy. But I'm heading home tomorrow.*

Piper: *That's either good or bad.*

Lane: *It's good. I got everything done that I needed to.*

Piper: *Good. What are you doing tonight?*

I hesitated, trying to figure out how to answer. I had a feeling she was genuinely curious, but past relationships had taught me that she might also be making sure I wasn't with someone else. I wanted her to trust me—I only wanted to be with her, and her dog, of course.

I waited a few seconds before responding, but as I typed, I saw the three dots pop up on the screen, disappear, then return. My heart pounded in my chest. Then the message came through:

Piper: *Can you tell your doorman to let me up?*

Lane: *What?* (That didn't make any sense. She was here?)

Piper: *Please. Your sister gave me your address, and I left this afternoon. I couldn't go another day without talking to you.*

. . .

I immediately called the doorman to ask if a beautiful brunette woman, about five feet six, was there. He confirmed it, and I told him to hold her there—I was on my way down. I rushed out of my apartment without shoes, pounding the elevator button over and over, praying it would hurry up. After what felt like a thousand years, the doors finally opened, and there she was, standing in the lobby.

Piper, in leggings and an oversized light pink sweatshirt, her backpack on her back, and a black crossbody bag slung over her front. Her hair was in a messy bun, no makeup, and she wore Birkenstock clogs with thick wool socks. I had never seen anything as beautiful as she was.

"Piper!" I couldn't help but call out. My deep voice echoed through the marble lobby, and she looked up at me, then quickly turned away from my doorman, who seemed to be engaged in a conversation with her.

"Lane!" she cried, running toward me. I expected to catch her in my arms, but as she neared, she slowed down. I could sense the hesitation in her body, though I couldn't figure out what was behind it. Her eyes looked wild, as if she was struggling with something.

"Lane," she said again.

"Piper," I said softly, my heart pounding. "What are you doing here?"

"I—I..." She looked away, her thoughts clearly racing. She stood there, contemplating her words for a few seconds, before turning back to face me. She took a deep breath and blew it out, then another one. I could see her trying to calm herself, and it was adorable.

She closed her eyes, blew out another breath, and finally began her monologue.

"Lane, I missed you. The day isn't even over, but I couldn't go another one without talking to you. I felt sad when you left this morning, and I knew you'd be back. I thought I could wait to see you, wait to figure things out. But then I realized I was being an idiot. I shouldn't have ignored talking to you for so long. So my first thought was to show up and do some big rand gesture, you know, like hold a boombox above my head and apologize. But then my adult brain kicked in, and I figured I'd show up in comfy clothes instead. I ate at my favorite sushi place, saw a friend who owns a wine shop, scoped out a bookstore, had a gin and tonic at the bar down the block... and then, I finally gathered the courage to come here."

I just stared at her in awe. She was here—adorably rambling about her day. The love of my life was standing right in front of me.

"But Lane, I missed you," she continued, her voice trembling. "And I hurt both of us by not speaking to you sooner. I jumped to conclusions, and I shouldn't have. I repeated the same mistakes instead of leaning in and communicating. I think I was just scared. I don't want to get hurt by you again."

Her deep brown eyes shimmered with emotion. I couldn't find the words, so I just stepped forward and wrapped my arms around her, kissing the top of her head over and over.

"Piper," I whispered, "I'm scared too. But I love you, and I'm not going anywhere. I meant it when I said it this morning, and I'll say it again so you know for sure: Pine Hills, Bennett's, my loft there, you, Sasha... *you* are my home."

She clung to me, and I kissed her again. "Now, let's go upstairs to my apartment. You'll hate it when you see it."

CHAPTER SEVENTEEN
PIPER

He opened the door, and I stepped inside after him. The apartment was enormous and very white—everything was pristine, almost too perfect. Sasha would stick out like a sore thumb in such a space. Her black fur would ruin all the rugs, the furniture—everything. The place was so luxurious, it felt like I was stepping into a hotel's penthouse.

"Damn, Schiller. This place is nice. You must be a multi-millionaire," I said, half-joking.

"I got a steal on it. It came fully furnished, and it's owned by a buddy of mine, a multi-billionaire." He smiled, but I wasn't sure I believed him. He had the look of someone who *was* wealthy, even if he was playing it off. "Can I get you anything to drink, Pipes?"

"Oh! I brought wine. Well, my friend gave me wine." I shrugged off my backpack and pulled out a bottle of expensive Cabernet Sauvignon. My car was stocked with bottles from her— she always made sure to send me with a few of her favorites when I visited. I handed Lane the bottle, and he quickly got to work opening it.

"So, Piper, sounds like you had a busy day," he said as he

poured wine into two beautiful stemless glasses and came around the island to hand me one. "Why don't we go sit on the couch? You can tell me all about it."

I froze, suddenly uncertain. "Lane, I think it's safer to stay here at the island. I have a feeling I'm going to spill this red wine, and I'd hate for it to end up all over the pristine furniture."

He laughed softly. "Fair enough. You've always been a bit of a klutz."

I "pshed" at him and stayed put on my stool, my gaze fixed on the wine in my glass. He sat on a stool beside me, and we faced each other, our knees brushing.

"So, Pipes," he said, his voice softening. "Tell me what's on your mind."

I hesitated before speaking, my hand resting on his. "I've been thinking a lot about how I overreacted the other day."

"Okay. Well, let's talk it through. But first, I want to say I'm so sorry, Piper. I never meant to hurt you—"

I cut him off gently. "Let me start, Lane." I stared at him, my hand on top of his. "Please forgive me for overreacting. I didn't give you a chance to explain. I should've asked you about that conversation instead of jumping to conclusions. Instead, I let all the anger I've carried toward you for the last 15 years take over."

"Thanks, Pipes." He sighed, then looked at me with such sincerity. "I'd like to explain if that's okay?"

I nodded, my eyes never leaving his. He started telling me everything—the pressures of his job, how his editor had mentioned the other woman, and the struggles he'd been facing in the last few days. He even confessed how he had wanted to knock on my door multiple times, to corner me in the bookstore, but had restrained himself, knowing he couldn't push me. I could feel his honesty in every word, and I appreciated it more than he knew.

For a moment, sadness crept in. I was angry at myself for

acting like a fool. I was a grown woman, and yet I had let old habits take over, acting more like a teenager than someone with my years of experience.

"Thanks for explaining, Lane," I said, my voice quiet. "I really appreciate it. And I'm sorry again for how I reacted. Especially when the few nights before that had been so amazing. I love you. But I'm scared. Will you give me a second chance?"

His expression softened, and he reached for me, pulling me close. "I love you too, Piper. And of course, I'll give you a second chance. Isn't this technically our third attempt though?"

I smiled, the warmth in his words reaching deep inside me. He leaned in and kissed me, and the passion in that kiss set me on fire. Without warning, he stood and lifted me off the stool, his hands gripping under my thighs. I wrapped my legs around him instinctively.

"Are we okay now, Pipes?" Lane asked, breaking the kiss for a second. A spark of hope flickered in his muddy brown eyes. "Is the third time a charm?"

I nodded, my heart beating wildly in my chest. With that, he carried me to the bedroom, ready to begin our third chance at happily ever after.

CHAPTER EIGHTEEN
EPILOGUE: LANE

Three years later...

It was 2 p.m. on Christmas Eve, and Piper was finally shutting down Bennett's. She had planned to close at noon, but a steady stream of last-minute customers had kept her there longer. She kept saying she couldn't turn anyone away on Christmas Eve. I tried to help, but after my last book release and the fall reveal of my true identity, things had gotten crazy. My female readers went wild when they found out I was a guy writing romance. Bennett's also got busier once they learned I was back in Pine Hills. I had people constantly asking me to sign books. It was great for Piper and for the town.

Piper turned around after locking the door and came toward me, smiling as I smiled back. Over the last three years, I'd been constantly amazed at how lucky I was.

"Well, are you ready to go upstairs?" she asked, her face lighting up. "We can watch *Home Alone* and make some eggnog."

She looked beautiful in her ugly Christmas sweater, black leather pants, and tall boots. Her hair cascaded in long waves. I brushed a stray strand behind her ear. "You're the most beautiful woman, person, *thing* I've ever laid eyes on."

"You're the most handsome thing I've ever encountered." She grinned. "Tonight, I just want to relax. Maybe exchange gifts. I've got the best one for you."

"Sounds perfect to me." I was thrilled to give her mine.

I'd moved into Piper's apartment above the shop nearly three months after that night at my place. When I told my friend I'd be moving out and in with Piper, he was ecstatic. What Piper didn't know then was that Everett—the owner of the property—had gone to high school with us. He'd made it big as an investor and entrepreneur.

I didn't have much in my NYC apartment, so moving back to Pine Hills was easy. I stayed across the hall from Piper for a while, but it was kind of silly. We spent every night together at her place. After three months, Piper asked me to move in as a birthday present for her. She said it was the best gift she could ever get. We spent the next day moving my stuff over, including the desk she'd originally bought when she thought she'd be renting the HomeBnB to L. Schiller.

Since then, I'd written five more books, all inspired by her, our travels, and the people of Pine Hills. My career had skyrocketed. Piper had written her first children's book, which became a huge success. She even did a mini-book tour that coincided with mine, so we got to travel the U.S. together.

Piper had started letting her longtime staff member, Lola, mostly manage the bookstore while Piper learned the ropes of running the other businesses her grandparents owned. They were ready to retire, and I was helping more with the HomeBnB rentals. We'd expanded by renovating apartments above the other shops her family owned. Things were busy, but life felt full and good.

The apartment felt cozy as the night wore on. *Home Alone* was nearing the end, and the room glowed softly from the Christmas lights. Piper was leaning against me on the couch, Sasha sprawled out on top of her.

I slowly rose. "Hey babe, I'm going to take Sasha outside. Need anything?"

"Nope, I'm perfectly content." She looked completely at peace.

I leaned down to kiss her forehead. "We'll be back in a moment." Then to Sasha, "Let's go outside, girl." I needed to grab Piper's present from my car. This was the moment. Taking Sasha out was just an excuse.

Once I had the gift and Sasha finished her business in the little dog space I'd set up in the courtyard, we headed back inside. My nerves had kicked in. I didn't think I'd be this anxious giving Piper her present, but I was. What if she hated it? What if now wasn't the right time?

As I opened the door, I took a deep breath. Sasha bolted inside.

I glanced around and found Piper standing by the Christmas tree, staring at its beauty. She was holding a box, looking just as ready as I was to exchange gifts.

"What's that?" I asked, my voice teasing but soft.

"Your gift," she said, her voice quivering as she extended it to me.

"Funny, I had to grab yours too." I walked toward her, my heart pounding as I realized—this was it. She was my forever.

"Should we swap simultaneously? You want to go first? Or should I give you mine first?"

"How about I go?" I dropped to one knee. Piper gasped, her eyes instantly filling with tears.

"Lane, is this—?" She trailed off, unable to finish the question.

I nodded, my throat tight. "Piper, it is what you think it is. I've loved you my whole life. I loved you then, and I love you now. Our life is amazing, and I love *us*. And I sure as hell love our dog—because she's ours."

Piper laughed, tears streaming down her face.

"I want you to be my wife. I should've asked a long time ago, but with this third time around, I wanted everything to be perfect. Please, Piper, will you marry me?" A tear slipped down my cheek, and before she could answer, Sasha bounded in to lick it away.

We both laughed. Piper knelt beside me and wrapped her arms around me. "Yes, Lane. I'll marry you."

She kissed me softly, and then pulled away, her expression changing. "But before we talk about marriage, we need to discuss something else. It goes with my gift."

I sat up, curious. "Oh yeah? You have a gift for me?"

Piper scooted into my lap, sitting with me in front of the tree. Sasha, ever the attention-seeker, huffed and flopped down beside us. It felt like the world had finally fallen into place.

"I've been feeling a little off lately." Piper's voice was hesitant.

"I know. You mentioned going to the doctor. You thought your anemia might be back." I felt a wave of concern wash over me, dreading what she might say.

She saw the panic in my eyes. "You don't need to worry. I'm healthy, Lane. I'm fine. All I need to do is stay healthy."

She handed me the box she'd been holding, and I took it slowly, unsure. "Open it, Lane. It's not a bomb," she said, trying to lighten the mood, but I could feel her shaking in my lap.

I carefully opened the box, which was larger than I expected. Before I could rip the tape off, I took a deep breath.

Inside, another box. My curiosity spiked, and I glanced up at

Piper, who looked like she might pass out. "Are you okay, babe?" I asked, concerned.

"Open it, please. I need you to see what's inside and then... then I need you to tell me you still want to marry me," she said, her voice thick with nerves.

I opened the second box, looking back at her. "Piper, I love you. Nothing could stop me from being with you."

Inside the box was a pregnancy test.

I blinked. "What? Are we... are we...?" Tears welled in my eyes.

"We are." She grabbed my face with both hands, her eyes filled with emotion. "I know we've been careful, but... going off the IUD, switching to the pill, then the antibiotics I was on..."

Our lips met in a kiss, deep and full of emotion. I wrapped my arms around her and pulled her close. "So... what do you think? Now that we're expecting... do you still want to get married?"

She smiled, her eyes shining. Still, there was a trace of nervousness. She was waiting for reassurance, for confirmation that this was real, that we were really doing this.

"Of course," I said, my voice trembling. "I can't wait to build a family with you. To be your husband."

My laugh broke through the tears streaming down my face. "This is everything I've ever wanted—a life with you, a family with you, and Sasha by our side."

I cupped her face and kissed her again, pouring all my love and promise into it.

Sasha, our ever-loyal Newfie, decided she wasn't about to be left out. She nudged in between us, her tail wagging furiously, and licked both our faces.

We broke the kiss, laughing as we turned our attention to Sasha. "You're part of this family too, you know. Gotta be the big sister and protector," I said, scratching behind Sasha's ears.

She barked happily, almost as if she understood the weight of the moment.

My fiancée smiled at me, her fingers lacing through mine. "I think she's just excited about being a bridesmaid."

"She'll steal the show," I said, grinning. "No doubt about it."

We stayed there for a moment longer, wrapped in love and dog fur, the world outside forgotten. This was it—the beginning of the life we'd dreamed of: messy, joyful, and perfect.

CHAPTER NINETEEN

BONUS CHAPTER

SASHA

Mom was working herself to the bone again. Bone. Yum. Just thinking about it made my tail wag. Oh, wait, let me focus. Where was I? Oh, right—Mom. She was ignoring me again, too busy staring at her glowing box (I think humans call it a computer). Sure, the customers at Bennett's petted me, and I always rewarded them with as many kisses as possible, but it wasn't the same. I wanted Mom's attention—the good kind, the one-on-one pets and belly rubs she usually gave out like treats.

But lately, she'd been distracted. I knew it had something to do with the male human who lived across the hall. We ran into him sometimes, and every time he did, Mom got all flustered. I could sense it—she wanted to run, but where would she go? I liked him, though. When I first sniffed his butt, I knew he was a keeper. Calm, kind, and, I bet, good at belly rubs. But for some reason, Mom didn't see it.

Now it's been years—YEARS—with this man living right across the hall, and she still ignores him. And guess what? She's also been ignoring me! So what's a dog to do?

I had a plan. If Mom wasn't going to give me the attention I deserved, I'd go get it from him. That's right—Operation Love from male human was a go.

I got up, stretched (you can't rush greatness), and decided to check in on Mom one last time. Maybe she'd notice my adorable puppy-dog eyes and realize her mistake. I trotted to her office, sat down, and stared. Nothing. She barely glanced up, too busy with her glowing box. Fine. I'd show her who's boss.

On my way out, I stopped at the front of the shop. A nice grandma caught my eye. She smelled of... wait... was that food in her purse? Jackpot! I gave her my best nudge and wagged my tail like the good and gorgeous girl I was.

"Oh, aren't you a beautiful bear!" she cooed. Bear? No, ma'am, I'm a dog. A big, gorgeous, fluffy Newfoundland dog, thank you very much. She scratched behind my ears (my favorite spot—four paws weak every time), and I melted.

"I think I have a treat for you, sweetie." Oh, she was an angel! She reached into her purse and pulled out not one, not two, but THREE treats. I sat immediately, showing off my good manners. She smiled and handed them over, and I gently licked them out of her hand, swallowing them whole.

"You're the best part of this bookshop, sweet girl," she said before wandering off. I stayed put for a minute, basking in the glory of her compliments and treats. I had a small hope that she would come back and give me more. Then I remembered, I had a mission.

I headed upstairs to the male's door, my tail wagging with determination. If Mom wouldn't give me love, maybe he would. I scratched at the door. Nothing. I waited. Scratched again. Still nothing. Finally, after what felt like forever (okay, maybe ten minutes), the door opened.

"Sasha! My beautiful Newf, what brings you here? Need some love?" The tall man crouched down, his hands already reaching for me. Oh, he understood me. I leaned into him, and before I knew it, I was on top of him, licking his face in gratitude. My drought of no pets was over!

"Alright, alright!" he laughed, getting to his feet. "Come on in. How about some TV and belly rubs? Want water first?"

I barked happily, tapping my front paws to signal a resounding yes. He chuckled and fetched me a big bowl of water, which I guzzled down. Those stairs and treats really took it out of me.

"So, Sasha," he said, looking at me warmly. "I'm Lane. I figure if we're hanging out, we should be on a first-name basis. Want to watch something? Maybe *Bluey* or *The Secret Life of Pets*?"

I barked again, my paws pitter-pattering in excitement. We settled onto the couch, and I sprawled across his lap as he scratched my ears, belly, and head all at once. He was tall and, as Mom liked to say, muscular—definitely strong enough to handle the full weight of my big, *thicc* (I've heard humans say that with two C's), beautiful Newfie self. It was pure heaven.

As I drifted off to sleep to his pets and the sound of the T.V., I thought to myself, *This is the life*. Maybe I'd give Mom another chance later—but for now, Lane was my hero.

ACKNOWLEDGMENTS

Writing this novella was a spontaneous decision inspired by NaNoWriMo. I had been deep into writing my novel and needed a quick brain break from those characters and stories. Second Chance Christmas came as a surprise, but I felt compelled to write something uplifting. What better way to do that than with a Christmas romance?

Over the few weeks I spent writing this story, I devoted a lot of time and energy, often stepping away from the people I care about most. First, I want to thank my friends and family for their patience, immense support and understanding during this creative journey. Writing has always been my dream, and this year, it all started to fall into place.

To my sons, thank you for being my biggest fans. Cheering you on in your pursuits has been one of my greatest joys, and it's humbling and motivating to feel your support in return. Lastly, to my husband—thank you for being my constant cheerleader and the one who always pushes me to chase my dreams. Everyone needs a hype person, and I'm so grateful that your mine.

ABOUT THE AUTHOR

Laramie Cummings is a rising author who refuses to stay boxed into just one genre—her imagination knows no limits! By day, she navigates the fast-paced world of fintech, but off the clock, her life is a delightful juggling act. She's a proud mom to two rambunctious kids, a spirited partner to her husband, and the ringmaster to a quirky pet duo: a dog and a cat who's convinced it's one too. When she's not spinning stories or chasing the next big idea, you might catch her reading, skiing, or creating a coloring book.

ALSO BY LARAMIE CUMMINGS

<u>Coloring Books</u>

Color Wyoming

Detective Demi: A Coloring Storybook

<u>Pine Hill Series</u>

Second Chance Christmas

Love in the Stacks